Murder With a Swirl of Blueberry

An Ivy Clark Mystery

Kristy T Dixon

For Maddie and Grace

Chapter 1

"Perfect," I said, sitting back to admire the cupcake I just finished frosting. I was getting better at piping the frosting into intricate patterns. Perfect was a stretch. It was nowhere near perfect, but so much better than the last ones I'd decorated. "What do you think?"

Carrie came closer and inspected it. "It looks good. I think you've got it."

"Thanks for teaching me."

"I've always loved decorating. It's my favorite part of working here."

I nodded and started on another cupcake. It wasn't my favorite thing to do, but I felt proud of how it turned out. If I were faster, there would be more to brag about. The dinner crowd would start any minute, and I had frosted two, and Carrie had done ten.

The back door to the diner opened, and Livy rushed in, her red ponytail swinging. "Sorry I'm late," she said, pulling on a lavender apron. "My tire was flat."

"No problem," I said, keeping my eyes on my frosting bag.

"Hey, Ivy?" she asked.

I glanced up. "Yeah?"

"Are you going to the county fair?"

"I'm not sure. Probably."

"I paid to be a vendor. I was going to make jewelry and hair bows, but now something's come up, and I can't go."

"That's too bad," I said, not really paying attention.

"The booth space was a hundred dollars, and I lose it all if I don't sell it to someone. I was wondering if you might want to buy it from me."

"Your booth space?"

"Yeah. You could sell desserts."

"That might be fun," I said, squeezing out more frosting.

"Thank you!" Grabbing her notepad and pen, she rushed from the kitchen and into the dining area.

I stood and looked at Carrie. "What did I just agree to?"

Carrie grinned. "Pay Livy a hundred dollars and take over her booth at the county fair."

I groaned. "When's the fair?"

"It goes over the Fourth of July. It's Monday through Saturday. They do fireworks every night. The rides and animals are great. It's a lot of fun if you're into that sort of thing."

"Great," I muttered. "I wonder if I can get Anton to run it."

"I doubt it. Anton took next week off, remember? His family's going on vacation."

"Livy took next week off as well," José said from where he was cooking a burger on the stove. "I bet she's going with him."

I nodded and placed the cupcakes on a platter. The town book club was meeting tonight, and they had requested cupcakes.

"I thought it was so cute when Anton and Livy started dating, but it's getting annoying. They always take the same days off, and they're late about a third of the time now."

"Speaking of Anton," José said, "he's late."

The bell to the diner tinkled, and I glanced out the serving window. My face lit up, and I wiped my hands on my apron.

"Jett must be here," José said, giving me a sly smile. "Only the sheriff and your cat make your eyes sparkle."

I ignored him and went into the dining area. Jett stood near the door holding up a receipt, his eyes fixed on me. I walked over, and he handed it to me.

"What's this?"

"My dry-cleaning bill."

I tilted my head. "Okay?"

"Do you want to see my invoice from the carpet-cleaning people?"

I raised my brow. "Not really. Should I want to?"

"Conan does not want to be potty trained. It's been weeks. I thought you might want to reimburse me."

I smiled and led him to a table. I'd gotten him a puppy, and he was turning out to be a lot of work. Jett sat down and sighed.

I sat across from him. "I'm sorry. I'll never give you a dog again."

He grinned. "I hope not. One's all I can handle."

I looked at his dry-cleaning bill. "Holy cow. How much dry-cleaning do you have?"

"All my uniforms."

"You should change the type you buy. Get all machine washable."

"I didn't notice when I ordered them, and I have a lot. I had them all cleaned, then I put them on the couch when I got home, and Conan did his business on them, so I had to take them again."

"That sounds like a you problem," I said, trying to look serious. "You should have hung them up. Don't blame the cute puppy."

"That's what Boyd said."

"Where is Boyd? I haven't seen him today."

"He's helping Barbra with something at her house."

"Can I get you some food? I'll give it to you for free to make you feel better about your dry-cleaning bill."

He took my hand from across the table and kissed it. "I'm just teasing you about the bills. I'll pay for my food. I have something for you." He pulled out a small box and opened it. A gold bracelet with golden bangles dangling down sat in the box.

I smiled. "That's the one I saw when we were in Wichita last month."

"Yeah, I went back the next day and got it. I was going to save it for Christmas, but I couldn't wait that long."

He handed it to me, and I slipped it on. "Thank you. I love it." I held out my arm and admired it. "Are you going to the fair? I just volunteered to do a booth."

"Yes. I stay most of the time for security."

"What should I sell?"

"Cheesecake?"

"It might not do well in the heat, but I could try."

"Do cheesecake and cookies. That way, you can make tons of cookies, and you won't have to worry about running out, but you still have something fancy. You can take some big coolers to keep it in."

"I don't know how I'm going to run a booth and keep up with the diner. Livy and Anton will both be off. I might see if I can trade out with José and Carrie. I agreed because I wasn't paying attention."

"Were you frosting cupcakes?"

"Yeah, why?"

"Because whenever you're frosting cupcakes and I'm talking to you, I can tell you aren't listening."

I wrinkled my nose. "Are you sure?"

He grinned. "Positive. José and I were testing you the other day. We were both trying to see what crazy things we could say without you noticing."

My lips turned up. "Sorry. Making pretty frosting is hard."

He laughed. "It's okay. We were having fun."

"When do you get off?"

"I just did."

"Do you want to eat upstairs?"

"Sure."

"What do you want? I'll have José text me when it's done."

"Burger and fries."

I hurried into the kitchen and gave José the order, then told him I'd be in my apartment. I lived above the diner, which was nice when the weather was bad, but there were some downsides. I felt like I was always at work.

Jett and I went up and sat on the sofa while we waited for the food. I kicked off my shoes and put my feet on the couch. Creepers wandered lazily into the room and jumped up next to me.

I ran my hand over his back. "Hey, buddy." He meowed and curled up against me.

"I can probably help you with your booth," Jett volunteered. "If you need to take a break or anything, I can guard your stuff. I'm usually pretty bored there."

"Are there lots of people?"

"Not like the state fair, but it's still a pretty good size. The fireworks shows are huge, so that brings in a crowd."

I pulled my blond hair over my shoulder and began braiding it. "I hope so. I'm paying Livy a hundred dollars for the booth."

He raised his brow. "One hundred dollars? A day, right?"

I frowned. "I thought it was one hundred for the entire week."

"I doubt it. My mom had a booth one year, and it was fifty dollars a day, and that was a long time ago."

I groaned. "I'll have to sell a lot of cheesecake."

"I believe in you."

"How's work?"

"It's been slow lately. That's a good thing, though." He grinned. "It means you've been minding your own business."

"Ha-ha. I've been busy. I can't do your job for you all the time."

"Ouch."

I laughed. "You know I'm kidding. You're a great sheriff."

"When you told me you were going to help Barbra clean out her attic, I thought you would find a dead body and start investigating it."

I pulled Creepers onto my lap, then turned and leaned my back against the armrest. I put my stockinged feet on Jett's lap. "I've been so busy. We aren't doing anything with the attic until we finish cleaning out the rest of the house. It could take a year."

Jett shifted his position, then took one of my feet and began rubbing it.

"How's Deputy Russell?" I asked.

Jett let out a slow breath. "Not endearing himself to anyone."

"But he's not as bad as Deputy Ledford, right?"

Jett chuckled. "Ledford's growing on me. Deputy Russell has been here almost two months, and he's never where he's supposed to be. Everyone he's dealt with has filed a complaint because he's rude."

"He's always nice when he comes into the diner."

"That's because you're attractive, and you're giving him food."

"In my opinion, if Ledford can grow on you, anyone can."

"Ledford annoys people, but at least he works hard. Russell needs to be babysat. It's a good thing Jane works in the office. She watches him and isn't afraid to call him out."

I smiled. "I like Jane."

My phone buzzed, and I pulled it from my pocket.

"Is the food ready?" Jett asked. "I can go get it."

"No," I said, reading José's text. "Someone wants to talk to me. That usually means a complaint."

"I'll come with you."

Creepers meowed when I put him on the couch. He doesn't like being disrupted when he's comfortable. I slipped my shoes back on. "I know, kitty, but you shouldn't complain. I had half a foot rub. Now my left foot is going to be jealous."

Jett grinned. "I'll get the other one after dinner."

"I won't forget."

"I know."

We walked down to the diner and around the corner. I saw two people standing by the entrance talking to Livy. My smile dropped when I recognized them. I stepped back behind the wall, and Jett came with me.

"What's wrong?" Jett asked. "Do you know them?"

I put my hands over my face and groaned. "That's Hanson Stevens and Brooke Richardson."

"Should that mean something to me?"

I dropped my hands. "I dated Hanson for a very short time, and Brooke is his best friend."

"Are we going to stay hidden?" Jett asked. "Livy will hunt us down if we don't come out soon."

"I don't want to talk to him. It'll be too awkward. Why would he come here?"

Jett shrugged. "Come on. Better to get it over with than to stress about it."

He was right.

"How do I look?" I asked, touching my hair.

Jett gave me a crooked smile. "Beautiful, but why do you need to impress your ex?"

My mouth turned down. "I don't want Brooke to have any reason to judge me. She's… not that nice."

I took a deep breath and walked back out, with Jett a step behind me. Livy pointed at me, and Hanson and Brooke both turned and smiled. Brooke's smile was one hundred percent fake. She never liked me, and I'd always suspected she had a secret crush on Hanson.

I put on my own fake smile as I walked over to them. Hanson rushed over and picked me up, spinning me around. He placed me on my feet, and I tried not to roll my eyes.

"Hey, Hanson. Brooke. What brings you here?"

Hanson grinned at me and pushed his shaggy brown hair from his eyes. "We were on a road trip and thought it would be fun to surprise you. I thought you would be more excited."

I blinked. There was no reason for Hanson to think I would be happy to see him.

"I told you it was a bad idea," Brooke said, flipping her long black hair over her shoulder.

"We're staying at the B&B for a while. We heard there was a fair going on next week, so we thought that might be fun. You should go with us."

"I have a booth there."

"Great! Maybe we can do lunch."

"I'll be busy with the booth."

"You have to have lunch." He looked behind me. "Can we help you?"

I looked over my shoulder. Jett stood there with his arms crossed.

"Sorry," I said. "This is Sheriff Jett Malone. Jett, this is Hanson and Brooke. They're from my hometown in Arizona."

Jett shook their hands. "Welcome to Muddy Creek."

"Can we get a booth?" Hanson asked. "It's cool that you own the place."

"I'll have Livy help you. I'm busy so I won't be able to stay and talk."

"We can catch up tomorrow. We have time."

I nodded and left as quickly as I could. When I got upstairs and went to close the door, Jett was behind me. I'd almost forgotten about him in my desperate attempt to escape Hanson's company.

We went back to the couch, and I sank down on it. "Why did he have to come? This is going to be a disaster."

"Who broke up with whom?" Jett asked, grabbing my leg and pulling off my shoe. He started rubbing my foot.

I sighed. "It was a mutual decision, but I suggested it."

"How long were you together?"

"Three weeks."

"That's nothing."

"Yeah, I don't know why he would come here. It was a long time ago, and we haven't talked since. I even blocked him from my social media. Now I'll have to avoid him until he leaves."

"Just talk to him and see what he wants."

"I'd rather not."

"Why did you dump him?"

"I never should have dated him to begin with. He gets angry when anything goes wrong. When he screamed at a stoplight, I knew I couldn't take him anymore. I was glad it hadn't gotten serious. He called me a few times after, but I didn't answer."

"So if you stop taking my calls, I know I'm history?"

With a smile, I pulled my foot back and kneeled on the couch in front of him. I ran my hand through his brown hair. "You'll never be history."

He grinned and pulled me next to him. "Good to know." I cuddled into his side and hoped Hanson would decide to leave in the morning.

Chapter 2

T he cookies smelled delicious. Some people had drinking problems. I had a cookie problem. I made them all the time and never tired of them. I pulled the pan from the oven and placed them on the island. Thinking about cookies was more pleasant than thinking about Hanson staying in town. I'd managed to avoid him for two days, and I wanted to keep it that way.

"Hey, Ivy?" José said. "Your old beau and Jett are out there sitting at the same table."

I grumbled under my breath. I grabbed some cookies from the cooling rack, placed them on a plate, and went out with a phony smile. Hanson and Brooke sat on one side of the booth, and Jett sat across from them. Brooke was watching Jett, much too close for my comfort.

I'd met Brooke before Hanson. We had a mutual friend, and somehow all ended up at a dinner party at the same time. Brooke was nice enough until Hanson asked me out. He'd done it in front of her, and I'd seen the rage in her eyes. I should have said no. It would have saved me time and awkwardness.

I placed the cookies on the table and pushed my way in next to Jett. "Hello."

Hanson grinned. "Ivy! You're a busy person. I've been trying to talk to you for two days. They always tell me you're indisposed at the moment."

"Running a diner is a lot of work."

"I guess so if you don't have time for friends."

My eyes narrowed, but I kept my smile. "I'm afraid we aren't going to have a lot of time to catch up. I'm completely scheduled for the rest of the month." I was lying, and I only felt slightly bad about it.

"Can we just go somewhere and talk for a minute?"

"I don't think so. I need to go back to the kitchen."

Hanson turned to Jett. "Ivy and I dated a while back. That's why I'm really here. I don't think we gave it a good enough chance. What do you think, Ivy? I've missed you."

I rolled my eyes. It was just like Hanson to bring it up in front of people. Of course, I hadn't given him a chance to talk to me in private.

Jett placed his arm around me. "I'm opposed to that."

Hanson's eyes went wide. "Oh. I didn't realize you two were a thing."

Brooke smiled. "Well, I guess we can go home."

"No," he said. "I want to give Ivy time to think. Ivy, you have options. I want you to think about us. I'll give you a week."

I let out a small laugh. "I don't need a week. I'm with Jett."

"You didn't even take any time to think. At least sleep on it."

"Hanson," I said, trying not to sigh, "what we had was nothing. It only lasted a few weeks. I'm in love with Jett. Completely."

Jett squeezed my shoulder.

"Wasn't it a fun few weeks, though?" Hanson asked, ignoring the fact that I was sitting here with my current boyfriend. "Remember when we went to that outdoor theater?"

I stood. "I have to get back to work. If you stay, I'm not spending time with you."

Brooke had a slight smirk on her face. I couldn't understand how Hanson had never realized she liked him. I'd tried to tell him once, and he acted like I was crazy.

I went into the kitchen and over to the cookie sheet. After grabbing the spatula, I tossed the cookies on the cooling rack. Jett came in and sat on a stool and watched me.

"You're going to break all your cookies."

I let out an annoyed breath and tossed another. Jett reached over and took the spatula from me, then carefully placed the remaining cookies on the rack.

"You can't avoid him forever," he said.

"He isn't staying forever."

"I think you need to talk to him."

"I did when we broke up. I don't see a reason to do it twice."

"He's planning on going to the fair. He might hover around your table until you pay attention to him."

I sighed. That was exactly something Hanson would do.

José looked over from where he was cooking. "I can tell him to get lost. Just give me the word."

I smiled. José was in good shape, and he was good at intimidating people when he wanted to, but Hanson wasn't the type to take a hint, even when it wasn't a hint. He could be told something straight out and still think someone meant something they didn't say.

"Thanks, José. I've got it."

Jett's eyebrow rose. "Do you?"

I was saved from answering when the door opened and Boyd came in. "I smell cookies." He walked over to the island and frowned. "What happened to those?"

Jett grinned. "Ivy was taking her annoyance out on them."

I grabbed one of the slightly broken cookies and stuffed it in Jett's mouth. His eyes sparkled as he chewed.

Boyd took a cookie and turned to me. "Jett said you have a booth at the fair."

"Yep."

He scratched his bald head. "I usually avoid the fair, but I might come this year. I love the animals, just not the crowds."

"I'll need some help," I admitted. "It's long hours, so I'll need to take breaks."

"I can help," he volunteered. "What are you selling?"

"Cheesecake and cookies."

"I can switch out with you a few times," José said. "As long as it's a time when Carrie is here to hold down the fort."

"I have no idea how to plan," I said. "I'm afraid I'll make too much or not enough. I've never done something like this."

"I'll run some numbers for you," José said. "I can get you a fairly accurate estimate."

"Thanks, José."

Making José the diner's manager was the best thing I'd ever done for this place. He always had an idea, and he knew what he was doing.

"Did you leave Conan in the house?" Jett asked Boyd. Boyd moved in with Jett a while back and enjoyed playing with animals. He was Creepers's favorite person.

"No. I brought him and left him in Ivy's apartment."

I frowned. I didn't want a half-trained puppy in my place, and I still didn't trust Conan and Creepers to be left alone together.

"You better watch it, or Ivy's going to take your key," Jett said, grinning.

I'd given Boyd a key so he could play with Creepers during the day while I was working. I'd already regretted it a few times.

"Don't worry. I'm only going to be a minute, and then I'll go up with them. I just needed a pile of cookies."

I grabbed a baggie and handed it to him. He put a few in and sealed it. "Thanks."

"He gets an entire bag?" Jett teased.

I smirked. "I don't think you can complain. You eat the same amount as Boyd."

"I know, and I'm feeling it," he said, rubbing his flat stomach. "I have to do extra crunches every day just to make up for it."

"I'll go up with you," I told Boyd. "I haven't seen the puppy in days. Let's go out the back way."

Jett tilted his head. "You can't hide forever."

"Hide from what?" Boyd asked.

"Ivy's ex is out in the dining room."

Boyd's eyes lit up. "I heard he was here. Let me get a look at him."

"Boyd…" I said as he peeked out the serving window.

"Not bad," Boyd said. "He's attractive."

"And annoying. Let's go."

"Don't worry, Jett," Boyd said. "You're better looking, and you could take him in a fight."

Jett smiled. "Thanks. I was getting worried."

Boyd grinned at me. "Don't you want to introduce me to him?"

"Not at all."

I convinced Boyd to go upstairs with me, and I sat on the floor and let Conan jump on me. He's the cutest little ball of fluff I've ever seen. Jett had wanted a big dog, but this one was so cute, I'd been impulsive.

Boyd sat on the sofa, and Creepers came lazily over and sat on his lap.

"I'm going to make a police dog of Conan yet," Boyd said.

Conan spun in circles on my lap and yapped. I wasn't seeing it.

"I remember when you wanted to make Creepers into a police cat."

"I haven't given up on that. Retirement is boring. I need things to keep me occupied. Are you going to tell me about that old boyfriend?"

"No. I wish he would leave."

"So does Jett."

"He seems mellow about it. He keeps telling me to talk to him."

"That's because he thinks that's the right thing to do. And he thinks if you talk to him, he'll leave faster."

"Did he say that?"

Boyd rubbed his goatee. "Not exactly. He was ranting about the guy last night, but I tuned him out after a while."

"Hmm." Jett had acted completely unbothered around Hanson. It made me wonder what he was thinking. I try not to be jealous, but I would be uneasy if one of Jett's old girlfriends came by.

"I bet cheesecake is hard to transport," Boyd said, changing the subject.

"I have some coolers I can use to keep them cool." I stood and went to the kitchen and pulled out a large display... thing. I wasn't sure what to call it. It was made of stone, and was round and heavy. It was also polished and fancy, so I didn't use it much. I planned to put a display cheesecake on it for the fair.

"I have this," I said, walking back out to Boyd. "I'm going to put it on my table just for show. I won't sell the cheesecake I put on top."

"That looks heavy."

My muscles felt like they were bulging from the weight. "It is. I only use it if I don't have to move it around a lot. I have a glass top I can put over it so the bugs don't get to it." I took it back to the kitchen. If I was going to make over a hundred dollars a day, I needed all the advantages I could get. I needed my display to be eye-catching because I'm not the type to call out to people.

"I bet you make a lot."

"I hope so. I paid a lot to do this. Are you coming to Zumba?"

Boyd let out a long moan. "I thought I would be able to get out of it with the fair."

"I cancel so much I feel bad. That's why I'm doing it tonight. You always complain about it being too early, so this should be better."

"Any time I exercise, I'm going to complain."

"I need to go now, or I'll be late."

"I'm coming."

"Let me change, and we can go." I hurried and pulled on some yoga pants and a pink shirt, then we walked to the dance studio.

I loved teaching Zumba, but it felt like I always had something come up, so I ended up missing. Thankfully, my class was understanding. Most of them were only there for the social aspect, and they didn't actually want to work out.

"We were betting on whether you would show," Opal said when I opened the doors.

"Have I ever missed without sending a text?" I asked. I honestly didn't know. I'd gotten scatterbrained since I came to Muddy Creek. I was always too focused on something and missed other things.

"No," Barbra said. "Ignore Opal."

"I have something special today," I said. "I made a new playlist, and you all are going to love it."

"No playlist is going to make it less painful," Opal muttered.

"It's not painful," Barbra said, nudging her friend. "You just don't like to do anything."

I turned on the music and stood in front of the ten women and Boyd. The theme song from The Monkees blasted across the studio. Every song on the playlist was from way before my time, but I knew my class would appreciate it. I'd spent hours trying to figure out the best moves.

"I can get behind this!" Boyd said, kicking his leg out as he tried to copy me.

"I was in love with Davy Jones back in the day," Barbra said, mimicking my moves.

Opal shook her head and didn't even pretend to dance. "Micky Dolenz was better."

Part of the class danced, and the other part got into a small argument about who the best-looking member of The Monkees was.

When Simon and Garfunkel came on, I knew I'd made a mistake. Now the arguing turned to who caused the duo to break up.

I turned off the music. "If you're all going to argue, we're going back to my generation of music."

"We'll stop," Opal said. "Okay. No more arguing." I turned the music back on.

The glass door opened, and Brooke walked in. She wore a white tank top and shorts that barely counted as more than underwear. I ignored her and kept dancing. She smirked and put her large duffel bag in the corner. I couldn't imagine what was inside.

Boyd went over and talked to her. He'd made it his job to make sure everyone paid their monthly dues. I wouldn't mind someone taking a free class, but I didn't want Brooke here at all. She handed Boyd some money and began dancing.

I tried not to watch her, but my eyes kept going to her. She had a sly grin on her face. I couldn't tell whether she was making fun of me or trying to show off. She could kick high.

A few minutes later, Hanson came in. He sat next to the wall and watched. Now I got it. Brooke had come dressed like that because Hanson was coming. I normally don't let people watch because it makes me self-conscious, but I wasn't up for a confrontation.

When the session ended, my class went home. Boyd stayed to walk with me. Brooke grabbed her bag and grinned at Hanson. I turned off the music and grabbed my things.

"I didn't know the senior citizens did Zumba," Hanson teased. "Brooke was the only one under forty."

"How did you know about the class?" I asked.

Brooke slung her bag over her shoulder. "I overheard some people talking about it."

"I have to go. I have a big day tomorrow." I ushered them to the door and locked it behind us. Boyd linked his arm with mine, and we started for the diner. I could tell Hanson wanted to say something, but he kept quiet.

"I should teach a class like that," Brooke said, walking behind us. "There isn't a lot to it."

"You have to get certified," I said.

"I bet that's easy."

I decided to ignore her. Getting certified to teach Zumba hadn't taken long, but I'd made sure I was qualified. I'd taken extra training and gotten a few certificates.

"Why don't you do it?" Hanson asked her.

"I might."

Boyd looked over his shoulder. "Hey, Brooke? If you can't afford pants for Zumba, I'm sure we could get a few people to donate some money to help you out."

Hanson snorted, and Brooke smacked his arm. I held in a smile.

I tried to pull Boyd faster, but he liked to stroll and enjoy the air. I wondered what it would take to get Hanson to leave. I might have to sit down and have a conversation with him, but I wasn't up for that tonight.

When the road split and Hanson and Brooke went toward the B&B, I let out a relieved sigh. I wasn't going to
relax until those two left town.

Chapter 3

"Whoa, whoa, whoa!" I said as Boyd and I tried to stabilize my canopy at the fairgrounds. Jett had told us to wait for him, but Boyd had convinced me we could put it up without him. The canopy tipped to one side but didn't fall over. I pulled on the leg nearest me and clicked it into place.

"I think we've got it," Boyd said, clicking down his side.

"This is a lot of work," I complained, putting my hands on my hips as I studied the lopsided tent. "It doesn't look right."

"That's because you have one leg shorter than the others," Jett said, carrying a large tote over to us.

I pulled on the short leg. "It doesn't come out any farther."

Jett walked over and yanked on the leg. It extended and clicked into place. "I'll go get the table." Jett jogged off to the parking lot.

A man with a sandy-blond ponytail and a blue T-shirt walked toward us carrying a canopy. He looked familiar, but I couldn't place him. He dropped his canopy next to us and smiled. I would guess he was in his mid-forties.

"Hey. Looks like we're neighbors," he said. "What are the chances?"

I smiled and wondered where I'd seen him.

"Hey, Bill," Boyd said. "Selling your wood carvings?"

Bill nodded and kneeled to unzip the canopy bag. "Yep. This is my best event of the year. I should do well being next to you guys. Ivy will bring in the crowds, and people will look at my stuff while standing in line."

Now I felt really bad. He knew my name. He must be from Muddy Creek since Boyd knew him. I'd had a few awkward meetings with people I didn't know since I'd come to Kansas. Since I owned the only diner in town, people knew who I was, but I didn't always know them. I tried, but there was a lot of traffic at the diner.

Bill put up his canopy like a pro. He had it upright without any help. Jett came with my table and placed it on the ground.

"Hey, Sheriff," Bill said.

Jett nodded. "Hi, Bill. Selling your carvings?"

"Always. Are you patrolling the fair, or here for fun?"

"I'm patrolling. They have security as well, so it should be relaxed."

"That's good."

I opened my table and secured it in place, then covered it with a purple tablecloth I'd gotten for the event. I'd ended up spending a lot more than the hundred dollars a day to do this. If you counted the table, canopy, and decorations, I was out another three hundred and fifty. If we did well, I might consider coming next year since I had all the supplies now.

"Anyone need help?" Deputy Russell asked, walking up with his hands in his pockets. He had on black sunglasses and wore a cowboy hat.

"Nope," Bill said, his mouth turning down. "I'm good."

He looked at me. "What about you, Ivy Clark?"

I shook my head. "I think we're covered." Deputy Russell always called me by my first and last name. It made me glad he didn't know my middle name.

"Cool. I'll just do some laps around to make sure everything's in order." He walked off the way he'd come.

"That guy drives me crazy," Bill muttered.

"I needed to bring one deputy with me, and he was the only one who wasn't busy with anything," Jett said.

"I need to go get my table." Bill walked off.

"Who is he?" I asked.

"Bill Parsons," Boyd said. "I see him in the diner about once a month."

"That's why he looks familiar. I'm never going to learn who everyone in town is."

"And it's going to get worse," Jett said. "Did you hear they approved the condos for the town?"

"No."

"They're going to build a hundred condos. That will add to the population fast. At least if people buy them."

Boyd nodded. "I bet the first people to buy them will be people who already live in Muddy Creek. All of us older people want to live in town now."

"They're advertising part of it as a retirement community and the other half as family friendly," Jett said, pulling my stone cake stand from the tote. He put it on the table, and it made a thud. "That thing is heavy."

"Condos will bring me more business," I said. "I'm going to start unloading the food." I walked over to Jett's truck and tried to psych myself up. I'm not an introvert, but talking to lots of people I don't know isn't my thing. And trying to convince people they want to buy something? It was going to be a long week.

⚜

I stood across from my canopy, and my lips quirked upward. My display looked perfect. It would have to bring people over. I took a quick picture and looked at the time.

The ticket booth would open in ten minutes. The setup had taken a lot longer than I'd expected.

I sat on my folding chair and waited. Boyd had gone off with Jett, so I was by myself.

"Have you ever done a fair before?" Bill asked, sitting at his own booth. We'd tied the sides of the canopy up to let the breeze through and also so I could see the vendors to the side and behind me. I had a corner booth, so that made it less claustrophobic. I wondered if Bill would talk to me the entire week.

"No. This is my first time."

"Some events get boring, but not the fair. Once the gates open, you won't have time to think."

I looked at my coolers stacked behind me and hoped I had enough. I was selling cookies in individual bags and by the dozen. The cheesecake could be purchased in small individual plastic containers or in pie tins. I had the cookies out and ready, but I wouldn't bring out the cheesecake until people bought it. The display would have to be enough to tempt people.

It didn't take long before people began trickling in. The place was loaded within an hour, and I'd already made half my booth fee for the day. Jett had walked by a few times, but I'd been too busy talking to people for him to stop. I was going to run out, and what about the next five days? The fair ended late, so I would have to stay up all night to make enough.

I called José and told him what was happening. He volunteered to bake some more cookies and bring them to me. Carrie was going to make cheesecake that I could take tomorrow. Carrie's sister Tiffany agreed to go to the diner and help even though she wasn't scheduled to work today.

A few hours later, Jett slipped in behind me. "Go eat. I've got this."

I rushed through lunch, then walked around until I found Boyd. He was over by the animals, leaning against an enclosure.

"Look at those sheep," Boyd said when he saw me. "Did you know in some cultures sheep are symbols of prosperity, innocence, and peace?"

"I didn't know that." The sheep ignored everything but the hay they were munching on.

"Whoever came up with that didn't know sheep. We raised sheep when I was young, and nothing was innocent or peaceful about them. We had a ram that had it out for me when I was a boy. Every time I glanced in his direction, he took it as a challenge and tried to butt me over."

"So you don't like sheep?"

He chuckled. "I love sheep. I don't know anyone who doesn't need to be butted onto their head every now and again."

I wrinkled my nose. "They smell bad."

"You get used to it."

"Jett's at my booth. I better get back. I just wanted to make sure you were having fun."

"Yep. I'll come sit with you in a minute. I haven't seen the pigs yet."

"Take your time."

I went back and sat next to Jett. The line was gone, and there wasn't anyone at the booth. Everyone must be looking for food and not desserts for lunch.

"You're going to make all your money pretty fast," Jett said, standing. "You might run out of cookies."

"José and Carrie are baking for me. I'm going to have to give them a bonus."

"I better go walk around. I haven't seen Deputy Russell walk past, so I think he's slacking somewhere."

I watched him disappear into the crowd.

"This is the best I've ever done in one morning," Bill said. "I'm going to request to be next to you every year."

I laughed. "It might be you bringing people to me."

"Nope. People can't resist a good cookie."

My smile slipped when I saw Hanson walking to my booth. He had on a yellow polo shirt and tan shorts. Brooke wasn't with him.

"Hey, beautiful," he said. "Did you save me a cookie?"

I raised my brow. "If you pay for it."

He pulled out a dollar and set it on the table. Cookies were closer to four dollars, which my sign clearly stated.

Since I didn't want to waste time dealing with him, I took it and handed him a cookie.

He ran his hand over the side of my cake stand, then touched the glass. "I'm glad we can finally talk."

I pursed my lips as I tried to ignore the fingerprints he left. "I have nothing to say. It was nice to see you, but I'm not going to spend any time with you."

"That's harsh."

"I don't want to waste your time."

"Being with you isn't a waste."

"I don't want to be with you, Hanson. I don't even want to talk to you."

"Why?"

I rolled my eyes. "I don't like you." If that wasn't blunt enough, I didn't know what was.

"You think that sheriff is better than me?"

"Better for me. Why don't you ask Brooke out? You spent more time with her than me when we were dating."

"Is that what this is all about? I spent too much time with Brooke?"

"No. I don't care about that. Can you leave? You're scaring off business."

"Not until we get this ironed out."

"Hanson. Can you hear me? I'm done with you. It's been a long time. I've moved on, and you need to as well. Please leave."

"Is everything alright over here?" Deputy Russell asked, sizing up Hanson.

"Fine," he said.

"Ivy Clark?"

I forced a tight smile. "I need this man to leave."

"Got it," Deputy Russell said. He grabbed Hanson by the sleeve and pulled him away. Hanson shot me a dirty look as the deputy dragged him off.

"That was awkward," Bill said, pulling out a wooden chess set he'd carved. "Looks like you're trading up. Jett Malone is a good guy."

I ignored the heat traveling up my neck and just nodded.

A few minutes later, Deputy Russell came back. "I told him not to come back inside the fairgrounds."

"You didn't have to kick him out. I just wanted him away from my booth."

"I don't do warnings," he said. "If someone messes up, it's over."

Bill snorted, and Deputy Russell shot him a look. "Do we have a problem, Bill?"

"No."

"I didn't think so." He turned to me and grinned. "You know I have to uphold the law. Your booth is two inches farther out from the other booths. Give me a cookie, and I'll look the other way."

My eyes narrowed. "Wouldn't that be bribery?"

He laughed. "It's just a cookie, and I was joking."

I handed him a cookie and hoped it would make him leave. It did.

"I hate that guy," Bill mumbled.

I wasn't a fan either, but I would keep that to myself.

He came around his table and looked at my stand. "This display thing is nice," he said, touching the stone cake stand. "I bet it weighs a ton." He picked it up, then put it back. "That can't be fun to haul around."

"I don't use it much."

"It looks nice, though."

"Nice booth," an older man with gray hair and a security badge said. "I'm Perry. If you need anything while you're here, find me."

"Thanks, Perry. I'm Ivy, and this is Bill. He sells those neat wood carvings."

Perry nodded. "Very nice."

Deputy Russell came back over. "Hey, Perry. Trying to look important again?"

Perry's smile slid from his face. "Deputy Russell."

Deputy Russell looked at me and shook his head in pity. "These security guards are always trying to pretend they have power. In reality, they can't even carry a weapon so what good are they?"

"We keep an eye out," Perry said.

I smiled at the man. "I'm sure you do a great job."

Deputy Russell snorted. "A great job walking in circles and showing off his badge. He's a security guard. He doesn't do much." He turned and sauntered away.

"Ignore him," I said. "He's got issues."

"He's just a jerk," Bill said.

"I've worked with him before," Perry said. "He has something against security guards. He lets me know every time I see him."

"He feels self-important," Bill said.

"I believe in karma. He'll get his someday. I'll see you all later." He wandered away.

"Poor guy," I said.

Bill's forehead furrowed. "Russell has to make himself feel better by putting everyone else down."

"It seems that way."

I grabbed a paper towel and tried to wipe the fingerprints from the glass. Why did everyone feel the need to touch everything?

"Great," I muttered when I saw Brooke walking toward me. How many awkward conversations was I going to have today? She waited until Bill went back to his booth, then came over.

"Hanson said you had him thrown out."

"He got himself thrown out."

She narrowed her eyes and crossed her arms. "You need to have an honest conversation with him."

"I already did. I can't fix the fact that he doesn't listen."

"You think the sheriff is going to stay with you? Hanson's a loyal guy."

I laughed. "You want me to give Hanson another chance?"

Her lips formed a tight line.

"I didn't think so. He knows how I feel. I know how I feel. Now maybe you should let him know how you feel."

She tapped her fingers against her arms. "What are you talking about?"

"You like Hanson. You have since I met you. Tell him, or nothing is going to happen."

"No one can measure up to you in his eyes. And now you get to break his heart and move on to greener pastures. One day, you'll lose the things you care about, and you'll know how he feels."

"I never did anything to you. I don't know why you've always been so rude."

"You never should have dated Hanson. It lasted less than three weeks and left him hurt. If it was only going to last that long, you shouldn't have ever let it happen."

"I didn't know it would be like that. Should I have dragged it out and made it worse?"

She shrugged and walked away.

"Being next to you is far from boring," Bill said.

I took a deep breath and let it out slowly. Boring was definitely not my life.

Chapter 4

I didn't want to spend too much time away from my booth, so I jogged when I took a bathroom break. Boyd was watching my table, and I wasn't confident about his ability to take credit card payments. I'd shown him three times, and he still seemed confused. If I didn't hurry, he would probably end up giving away free food.

On my way back, I stopped dead in my tracks when I saw Jett sitting on the platform of the dunking tank. He had on his tan pants and sunglasses, but he'd thrown off his shirt and shoes.

He waved at me.

"Come dunk the sheriff!" the barker called out. "I've got Sheriff Jett Malone up here! Do I have any takers?"

"Is this how you protect the fair?" I teased, walking up to Jett.

"It's Barbra's and Opal's fault."

I grinned. "Oh yeah?"

"The man in charge was looking for volunteers, and Barbra and Opal spotted me and volunteered me. I guess the regular guy is at lunch. It's just for a half hour."

"Where did Opal and Barbra go? I would think they would be here waiting to watch you fall?"

"Barbra left her purse in the car. I'm sure she'll be back. I hope she has bad aim, but knowing Barbra, she'll probably hit the target on the first try."

"You're going to be soaked for the rest of the day."

"It's hot out here. I'll dry. Is your cheesecake melting?"

"Nope. I'm keeping it cold."

His shirt and shoes sat on the ground near my feet. I picked it up and shook my head. His gun and wallet were wrapped up in his shirt. That didn't seem safe. "You put your stuff right where all the water's going to splash."

"I didn't think of that." He pointed at his hair. "I'm dry so far."

I smiled and felt my eyes sparkle.

"I know that look, Ivy Clark. I also know I played Frisbee with you once, and I doubt you can hit anything with a baseball."

I tilted my head. "I accept your challenge."

"Don't waste your money."

I grinned and looked around, spotting Deputy Russell. I handed him Jett's things.

"Will you hold these?" I didn't think I could give them to just anyone, especially the gun.

He smirked. "Sure. I'd love to see this."

I went up to the barker who was calling out to the fair patrons and handed him enough money for three balls.

I took the first ball and smiled.

"Everyone, come see!" the barker called. "Is she going to dunk the sheriff?"

A crowd began gathering around, and all the self-consciousness I possessed flooded my body. I'd never been great at sports, so I didn't need an audience. I threw the first ball and missed the target by half a foot.

"Nice throw!" Jett called out.

"You can do it!" someone yelled.

"Do it for me!" a man called. "Get him back for my parking ticket!"

"Hey," Jett protested, "you can't park on the sidewalk, Harold."

"I was only halfway on the sidewalk!"

"Halfway is too much. I gave you a warning first."

"I'd still like to see you dunked!"

I threw the second ball. It hit the edge of the target, and Jett laughed.

"Dunk him! Dunk him!" Deputy Russell chanted. Soon, everyone in the area was chanting.

"Get Sheriff Jett!" a kid yelled.

"Traitor!" Jett said, pointing at the boy. The boy giggled. People loved Jett.

"Go, Ivy!" Barbra said.

"She should get to go closer," Opal said. "That distance is too far."

"I think I'm going to need more balls," I muttered. I threw the third ball and clipped the target. The crowd groaned.

"I'll pay for more!" a man said, handing the barker some bills. Everyone clapped. I wondered how pink my face was. I'd always hated being the center of attention.

Jett held his arms in the air. "If she makes the next shot, I'll kiss her!"

The crowd roared their approval, and the barker laughed. He probably hadn't expected this kind of attention when Jett got up there.

I gave Jett my best glare. "Great!" I called. "Now I have to miss on purpose!"

Jett and everyone else laughed.

"Maybe if you try to miss, you'll hit it," Jett said.

My hands had gotten slightly shaky from the attention. I pulled my arm back and missed worse than the first time. A unified sigh of frustration sounded behind me.

"I'll give you another chance," Jett said.

"I want something better than a kiss," I teased.

Jett put a hand to his heart and pretended to look hurt. "What could be better?"

"A Chunky Charlie's Chili dog." That wasn't what I wanted, but I'd seen a food truck with that name, and it was almost dinnertime. The crowd laughed and called out.

Jett's eyes lit up. "You're on. And I get a kiss if you miss."

The audience was amused. I felt heat creep up my neck as everyone talked and laughed about the whole thing.

I took a deep breath and tried not to remember the humiliation of high school softball. I pulled my arm back and slammed the target. Jett fell into the water, and I almost plugged my ears. The cheering was so loud.

Jett popped up and wiped water from his eyes. I walked over, sure the smile on my face was ridiculously large.

"Fifth time's the charm," he said, grinning at me. He pulled himself out of the tank and wrapped his arms around me.

"Stop, you're making me wet."

"Kiss, kiss, kiss," the crowd chanted.

"That wasn't the agreement," I said. "He lost."

"I'll get you your nasty chili dog. The kiss is a bonus." He leaned down and kissed me. I was all too aware of the cheers.

"I'm next!" a woman shouted.

"Then me!" said another.

I pulled away and put my arm around his wet back. "He's done."

"I'm done?"

I raised my eyebrow. "Yes. Now grab your shirt and go buy me my chili dog."

❧

"Are you going to watch the fireworks?" Boyd asked from his seat next to me. "They should be starting soon."

"Do you think I should leave my booth?" I already felt guilty for how long I'd left Boyd earlier. He hadn't minded, but I shouldn't have let Jett buy me the chili dog. My stomach hadn't been happy since I ate it.

"Not many people are wandering around anymore, and most of the vendors are at least standing in the open to see them."

"I guess I could do that." My stuff was almost sold out anyway, and I'd made more money than I'd thought was possible. Even if someone stole the rest of the cheesecake and cookies, I would be ahead. We stood and went into the middle of the tents. Most of the vendors had gone farther up, so we joined them. My booth was still in sight, but only if I turned around and squinted. It was dark, and the only lights were small twinkle lights hanging on the canopies.

Jett came up behind us and draped his arm over my shoulders. "It's been a long day."

I leaned in and gave him a side hug. "It has. And there are still five more."

"I might make Ledford come tomorrow."

I groaned. "You better not do that to me."

He laughed. "I won't. Have you seen Russell lately?"

"Not since the dunk tank."

"He's supposed to be constantly circling, but every time I see him, he's goofing off."

I cocked my head. "Goofing off how? Sitting at the dunk tank?"

Jett grinned. "That was only a few minutes, and I didn't want to do it in the first place. Russell isn't even pretending to work."

"He does act like a teenager," Boyd said. "How old do you suppose he is?"

"He's forty," Jett said. "He worked for the police in Wichita for sixteen years before he came here."

"Why did he come?" I asked. Most law officers avoided Muddy Creek because it was so small. It wasn't until this year that Jett got anyone to come work with him. When the pay was finally raised, a few deputies and some office workers came.

"He had some trouble with his last job. I think he wanted to go somewhere no one knew him."

Boyd shook his head. "He's not doing well with his new beginning."

The fireworks started, and we watched for a few minutes.

I glanced at Jett. "You finally dried, I see."

Jett ran a hand over his pant leg. "It dried fast, but now it feels stiff."

"You better avoid that area for the rest of the fair. That barker would probably want you up there the entire time."

"I still can't believe you hit it."

"I have skills."

He raised his brow. "Skills? I think you had a bit of luck at the end there." He grinned slyly. "Or maybe the thought of kissing me gave you more motivation."

"It was the chili dog."

"I can't believe you ate that thing. It was huge."

"My stomach hates me for it."

"I had to go back up for Barbra and Opal. They hunted me down and asked the barker to let me go back up. I bet they both spent thirty bucks."

"They missed that much?"

He chuckled. "Nope. Barbra's actually pretty talented. She dunked me five times. Opal got me once."

"You didn't kiss them, did you?" I teased.

He kissed the side of my head. "What do you think?"

"I bet it's nice to know that if the sheriff job doesn't work out, you can work at the fair."

"I'm glad you have faith in me."

I gave him a hug. "You're the best sheriff. I'm going to go check on my booth. I don't want to leave it unattended for long."

Jett nodded. "I'll come with you. I need to do another round."

We walked carefully through the grass and over to my canopy. The ground was lumpy and harder to navigate at night.

I squinted. "Did someone take my display cheesecake?" I took out my phone and turned on the flashlight. "They did! They even took my stone cake stand. I shouldn't have left. Who steals cheesecake?"

"I'll hurry and look around," Jett said. "No one's going to be able to move fast with that thing." He turned on his flashlight and began walking down the pathway.

I shined my light over the table. Frosting was smeared all over the tablecloth. That cheesecake had been out all day in the sun. If someone ate it, they were going to get sick. I should have put it away.

I made it halfway around the table when something caught my eye. I focused my light downward and covered my mouth. Someone was on the ground, not moving.

"Jett!" I yelled.

He came running over, and I pointed.

He frowned and dropped to his knees. I moved around the front, not wanting to see anything else.

"It's Deputy Russell," Jett said. I cringed at the strain in his voice. "He's dead."

Chapter 5

I paced across my apartment floor. Creepers and Boyd sat on the sofa watching me.

"You should sleep," Boyd finally said. "Wearing a hole in the floor isn't going to make Jett come back faster."

I looked at the clock on the wall. It was just after two in the morning. Jett hadn't texted or called.

"You can go home," I told Boyd. "There's no reason for you to stay up."

"I'm not leaving you alone."

"Why? I'm fine. I just need to think. At least take Creepers and go rest in my spare room for a few minutes."

Boyd yawned. "I guess that wouldn't hurt." He put Creepers over his shoulder and vanished down the hallway. I knew Jett was with a bunch of other officers, but I was still nervous about him being out in the dark with a possible killer. Especially a killer who had already killed a lawman.

A few minutes later, a light tap sounded on the door. I rushed over and pulled it open. Jett stood there, looking exhausted. I pulled him in and led him to the couch. He sank down, and I sat next to him.

"Are you alright?"

He nodded. "Just tired."

I wrung my hands. "What happened? Did he eat my cheesecake and die? It was out too long."

He looked at me and blinked. "Even if it were the cheesecake, he wouldn't have just dropped dead. Someone hit him in the head with a heavy object."

"Did anyone see anything?"

"No. Everyone was watching the fireworks."

"What did they hit him with?"

He looked at me and frowned. "Your stone cake stand."

I put a hand to my heart. I was afraid of something like this. Why had I brought the dang thing?

"Don't look like that. It has nothing to do with you," he said. "There was cheesecake all over the place. It was even under the table, and someone had kneeled in it and smeared it around."

"Under the table?"

"Yeah. They must have killed Russell, then crawled under the table."

"What would the point of that be? No one was around."

"Maybe someone walked past? I don't know. I'm going to have to go in early tomorrow."

"Take me with you."

He sighed.

I rubbed his arm. "Are you shutting down the fair?"

"I'm not sure. I'll have to keep your area blocked off for at least tomorrow. Sorry."

"I don't care about that."

He leaned his head back and closed his eyes.

"Are you hungry?" I asked. "I can get you something."

"No. I just need sleep."

"Boyd's in the guest room."

"I'll take him home. I just need to rest my eyes for a minute."

It took all of two minutes for Jett's breathing to get deeper. I grabbed a blanket and placed it over him. I pushed him gently down to the couch, and he didn't stir.

I tiptoed into the guest room. Boyd was slumped across the bed, snoring. Creepers looked up at me from the foot of the bed, so I picked him up and carried him to my room. I got ready for bed and climbed under my cozy comforter. I should be exhausted, but I had a hard time closing my eyes.

Creepers crawled onto my legs and went to sleep. I forced my eyes to close, and the next thing I knew, a pounding sounded on my door. I frowned. It was the door from the diner. No one should be in there. I squinted at the sun shining in. Had I slept in long enough that the diner was open?

I got to my feet and pulled my pink robe over my pajamas. I opened the door to see Brooke. She wore a massive frown, and her arms were crossed.

"What is it?" I asked.

She went down one step. "Are you sick? It's nine in the morning. Don't you run a business?"

Nine? I'd really slept in. I wondered if Jett had gotten up and gone back to the fairgrounds.

"Can I help you?" I asked.

Brooke sighed. "There isn't a doctor in town, and Hanson is sick."

"So take him to another town."

"He can't leave the bathroom."

"Why are you coming to me?"

"You're the only person I know."

I stifled a yawn. "Go get him some medicine."

"I don't know where to get anything."

I rolled my eyes. The town was small. Anyone on the street could point her to the pharmacy.

"I'll get something and bring it over. Give me thirty minutes."

Brooke nodded and disappeared down the stairs. The last thing I wanted to do was help Hanson. I couldn't believe Brooke came to me since she hated when I was around.

I went into the living room. Jett was still sleeping. I went over and shook his shoulder.

"Jett?"

He moaned. "What time is it?"

"Nine."

He sat up quickly and put a hand to his head. "I need to go." He jumped up and looked at me. "Are you coming?"

"Hanson's sick. I told Brooke I would take her some medicine. I'll take it over, then meet you at the fair." I went into the kitchen and grabbed two muffins. "Take these."

He nodded and kissed me quickly, then left.

I hurried to my room and got dressed, then went to the pharmacy and picked up a few things that might help Hanson. When I was there, I realized Boyd was still sleeping in my guest room. He would figure things out.

Miss Medley greeted me at the door of the B&B. By greeted, I mean she glared at me while she held open the door. It always annoyed her when I knocked, but sometimes I do it out of habit.

"I'm looking for Hanson Stevens," I said. "I have some medicine for him."

"So take it to him," she said. One day, I was going to figure out why Miss Medley was so angry all the time. I didn't know if it was aimed at me or if she disliked everyone. I'd never heard anyone else talk about how grumpy she was, and gossip ran rampant in Muddy Creek, so I figured it was only me.

"Where's his room?"

"Number 2."

I nodded and went down the hall. I knocked on room 2 and waited. Brooke opened the door and ushered me in.

"It took you long enough."

"It wasn't in my plans. Here it is." I handed it to her.

"Is that Ivy?" Hanson called from behind a closed door.

"Yes," Brooke said. She opened the door and tossed the medicine in, then shut it. "I'm going back to my room," she said, brushing past me. "This is the worst vacation ever."

I paused when she left. If Hanson was really so bad off, he might need help. I didn't want to be the one to help him, but Brooke didn't seem to want to take on that role, either.

I looked around the small room. A bed stood on one side and a dresser on the other. Clothing was strewn across the floor, and the bed was unmade.

Something about the clothing drew my attention. I walked closer and kicked Hanson's yellow shirt, which he'd been wearing the day before. Something had been smeared across it. I squatted and took a closer look. My eyes narrowed. It was cheesecake. I turned over his shorts. Blueberry syrup and creamy beige cake had been smeared near the seams above the knee.

I went to the bathroom door and knocked. "Hanson?"

"Ivy? What are you doing here?"

"I brought the medicine."

"Thanks."

"Did you eat my cheesecake?"

He groaned. "I feel awful."

"You should. That cheesecake wasn't for eating. You gave yourself food poisoning."

"I didn't eat your cheesecake."

"It's all over your clothing."

"You aren't the only person in the world who makes cheesecake."

"Why would you steal my cheesecake?"

"I told you, it wasn't yours."

"Where did you get it, then?"

"I feel awful. Can you leave?"

I shook my head and left the room. I didn't know what Hanson had done, but I knew he had eaten part of my cheesecake and had crawled around in my booth space. What I didn't know was whether he killed Deputy Russell.

Chapter 6

I scurried across the field to the area of the fair that was blocked off by crime scene tape. After looking both ways and finding it clear, I went under and made my way to my canopy. I'd gotten a text from the fair committee telling me my area was off-limits but that I could use a different area. I didn't see a point since all of my things were part of the crime scene.

Jett stood near the canopy, talking to another law officer. When he saw me, he came over.

"Any clues?" I asked.

"Not obvious ones. We're having everything finger-printed."

"I'm not saying I think Hanson did it, but he definitely stole my cheesecake."

Jett rubbed the stubble on his chin. "Why would he do that? I mean, your cheesecake is great, but it's not worth killing someone for."

"I don't know what he did, but he's sick, and there's cheesecake all over the clothes he wore yesterday. That cheesecake had been out in the heat all day. It would make anyone sick."

"Did you take the clothes?"

"No. I thought about it, but you told me I have to stop doing things like that."

He tilted his head slightly. "Where were they?"

"On the floor of his room. Should I call José and have him go grab them?"

"No. I'll call Ledford and have him go over. Did you crawl under the crime scene tape?"

I lifted my chin and gave him a small smile. "I didn't crawl. It wasn't that low."

"I can't think of any reason Hanson would have to kill Russell. He didn't know him, did he?"

"No."

"I really don't believe someone would kill someone to get cheesecake."

"What if he was taking the cheesecake, and Deputy Russell interrupted him, and he got scared?"

"That's possible. That cake stand is ridiculously heavy. He might not have realized the damage it could do."

I glanced over at Bill's booth. "I bet Bill's not happy he can't get to his booth."

"Nope. They gave him another one, and we gave him his wood carvings, but he was mad he didn't have his table and tent. I can't let him take it until we make sure there's no evidence anywhere around."

"Did Bill see anything?"

"No, but he said he thought he felt something rub against his legs yesterday when he was talking to someone. The cheesecake trail goes from under your table to under his. It's possible the person crawled from your table to his when they were trying to get away. Bill left about five minutes after the fireworks started, so it would have had to happen right after you left your booth."

"Why was Deputy Russell behind my table?"

"Who knows? He did his own thing."

"Sheriff Malone?" an officer said. "Can you come over here for a minute?"

"Sure." He looked at me. "Don't go far."

I wandered back under the tape and walked down the rows of vendors until I saw Bill. He was selling things off an old table with no canopy.

"Hi, Bill," I said, giving him an encouraging smile.

"Hey. Bummer about the murder. Did you get another table?"

"No. I was up all night, so I'm not in the mood to sit at a table today."

"It stinks that it happened in your booth. I bet they confiscated all your stuff."

"For now. I didn't have anything important there."

"I'm just glad if someone had to go, it was Deputy Russell. When I first heard a lawman had been killed at your booth, I thought it was Sheriff Malone since he sat there when you took a break."

I hugged myself as a chill went over my arms. I was thankful it hadn't been Jett.

"You didn't see or hear anything?"

"I went home a few minutes after the fireworks started. I did tell the sheriff the murderer might have hidden under my table. I felt something brush against my legs while making a sale, but I ignored it since I was busy. I saw a lot of dogs, so I figured one had found its way under there."

"It's all unfortunate. I don't understand the motive. Someone stole my cheesecake, but that doesn't seem like a reason to kill someone."

He grinned. "I don't know. Your cheesecake is pretty awesome."

"Thanks."

"Hey, have the police looked into that guy Deputy Russell threw out yesterday? Even after he was thrown out, I saw him a few times, so he must have snuck back in."

"I think they will."

"He might be mad that Russell threw him out."

I nodded. I wasn't going to tell him about Hanson's cheesecake-covered clothes. I didn't know Bill that well, and I didn't want to give out information that the police might want to keep quiet.

I picked up a pawn from the chess set Bill had carved. "These look really nice. Does it take a long time to carve?"

"I've been doing it so long I've gotten fast. It takes me about ninety hours to make a set."

I raised my brow. "Wow." I wasn't sure if that was fast or not since I don't carve things. That must be what the five-hundred-dollar price he was selling them was for. That was a lot of work.

"I carve when I'm stressed. It helps me calm down." He walked around the table and showed me the queen. "It took me years to perfect the queen."

I took it and studied it. "The detail is amazing." I caught a glimpse of Bill's shoe and then turned to look at it. "Sorry about your shoes."

"What?"

"They have cheesecake on them. That must have happened when the person was hiding under your table." There wasn't a lot, but purple blueberry syrup had stained them.

"It's fine. These shoes are worn out anyway."

"Well, good luck with your sales. I'm going to walk around."

"Let me know if you ever want a chess set. I'll give you a discount."

"Thanks."

I wandered through the fair, looking at all the booths. I wasn't paying much attention to them because my mind was going fast. Something Bill said was nagging at me. He said he'd thought the man who died was Jett. It had been dark last night, and Jett had spent a lot of time at my booth. What if whoever had killed Russell had meant to kill Jett?

I tried to push the thought to the back of my mind, but it wouldn't go away. When I reached the crime scene, I'd had enough time to thoroughly freak myself out. I weaved my way through several forensic people and spotted Jett. No one questioned my being there. That meant anyone could come in and attack Jett if they wanted to.

Jett was on his phone, so I waited at a close distance. So much was going on in this small area. I was surprised they hadn't shut down the entire fair. People stared as they walked by, and some stopped to see what was happening.

"Did you see Boyd and José?" Jett asked, putting his phone away.

"As far as I know, Boyd is still sleeping at my apartment."

"They were here a minute ago."

I frowned. "Why? José should be at the diner."

"He probably brought Boyd."

I nodded. Boyd didn't like to drive.

"What's wrong?" he asked. "You look concerned."

I wrapped my arms around him and looked up. "What if the person meant to kill you?"

He put his arms around my back and tilted his head. "I wasn't anywhere near here."

"What if they thought Russell was you, though? You were at my booth several times yesterday. You and Russell have a similar build, and you were wearing the same thing. It was dark."

His brows came together. "I guess it's possible."

"Be careful, okay? Don't go anywhere alone."

"I'm always careful."

I raised one eyebrow. "I can think of a few times you weren't."

He kissed my nose. "Don't worry about me. I need to do some things. Why don't you go find Boyd and José?"

I released him and went back out into the crowd. It didn't take me long to find Boyd and José at a booth throwing balls at targets.

"Any luck?" I asked.

Boyd threw a ball, missing the target by a foot. "I was going to play until I beat José, but I'm smart enough to see it's never going to happen."

José laughed. "I played baseball in high school."

Boyd wiped his brow. "Yeah, but that was a long time ago."

José threw a ball and knocked down the target.

The booth attendant whistled. "I haven't seen anyone knock down as many as you. You can take any prize."

José turned to me. "Pick a prize."

"You won it."

"You've had a bad twenty-four hours." He grinned. "And what am I going to do with a pink stuffed hippo?"

"Thanks, José." I picked the pink hippo. It was huge. We walked over to the shade and sat at a picnic table.

"Creepers is going to hate that thing," Boyd said, pointing at the hippo.

"Probably."

"I took Creepers to Brian. I hope that's okay. I didn't want him to be alone all day, and I'd already asked him to watch Conan."

"That's fine. Creepers loves Brian." Brian was the town librarian, and he owned Creepers's mom. He was also the person I got Conan from. "I probably owe Brian. He watches Creepers almost every time I need someone to."

"He loves it," José said. He tilted his head, and his eyes pierced mine. "Spill it."

"What?"

"I've known you long enough to know something's going on in your head. Is it about the murder?"

I bit my lip. "I'm worried about Jett."

Boyd chuckled. "Jett can take care of himself."

I filled them in on Hanson's clothes and Bill's comment about thinking Jett had been killed. "Am I crazy to worry?" I asked.

José ran a hand over his black hair. "I don't think so. If it were your ex, I bet it was aimed at Jett. I had Tiffany fill in for me at the diner. I'll keep an eye on Jett."

"I can help as well," Boyd said. "Of course, I'm an old guy, so I'm not that helpful."

I smiled. "You've helped me lots of times."

"Yeah, but I've caused you problems lots of times too."

José smirked. "Just don't go climbing any trees or getting stuck in holes in the floor."

Boyd's mouth turned up. "Good times."

José grew serious. "You need to be careful, Ivy. If someone is willing to kill someone to get back together with you, you could be in danger."

"It might not have been Hanson."

"Are there any other suspects?"

"Not that I know of. Brooke, maybe."

"Who's Brooke?" Boyd asked.

"Hanson's friend. You made fun of her shorts? She likes him, but he doesn't know, and she can't stand me."

"Right. But why would she try to kill Jett?"

"To hurt me? I don't know. It probably wasn't her, but we shouldn't count anyone out yet."

"What about other people near your booth?" José asked.

"I didn't meet the person behind me. The guy next to me is Bill. He was gone before it happened. At least, according to him. I don't know him well."

"I've known Bill for years," Boyd said. "He's fun to talk to, but he's been in and out of trouble since he was a teenager."

"Great. Does that mean I have to put him on the list?"

"Why would he kill Russell?"

"He hated him for some reason. He was the one who told me he thought Jett was the one who died, so I doubt it was him."

"Unless he meant to kill Jett."

"He likes Jett."

"Right."

I squeezed the hippo. "The cheesecake on Hanson seems the most suspicious right now."

"And the fact he has a motive."

I yawned, and my jaw cracked. "I should go back to the diner. I'm not doing any good here."

"Carrie and Tiffany can manage," José said.

"I know, but without a table, I don't have much to do. Besides, it's book club today. I should make sure the party room is ready. If anything happens, you can call me, and I'll come back." The fair was only a thirty-minute drive.

Boyd slapped his forehead. "I forgot about book club! I better go back with you."

"Hello, Ivy." I looked up to see Perry, the security guard.

"Hi, Perry. How are things?"

He shrugged. "Things have been crazy, with the murder and all."

"Did you see anything?"

"No. I was making rounds, but I was over by the animals. It's too bad it happened, but I can't say I'll miss Deputy Russell."

"You aren't alone in that opinion," Boyd said.

"I'm sure. Well, I hope you all have a good day." He walked back the way he'd come.

"Suspect?" José asked.

I scrunched my nose. "Doubtful. He's not young, and look how slow he's moving. That cake stand was heavy, and I bet he would have struggled to do it."

"Us old guys can surprise you," Boyd said.

José watched the man turn a corner. "We should probably tell Jett, just to be safe."

"Tell him what? That Perry didn't like him?"

"Yeah. He might have a motive."

"I suppose," I said with doubt in my voice. Perry didn't take me as the type. "I better go. I'll tell Jett to call me if anything happens."

Chapter 7

I placed a pitcher of lemonade on the table next to a plate of cookies in the party room. Barbra stood at the head of the table, and nine other women and Boyd sat along the sides.

"I don't think we can properly argue this book," Opal said, patting her curly gray hair. "Since Mr. Dickens died when he was writing it, he can't tell us how it was going to end."

Barbra's eyes lit up. "That's what makes it fun. No one knows what was going to happen. It could have been anything."

I smiled and sat at the foot of the table. I didn't usually stay, but for this, I would. "Are you talking about *The Mystery of Edwin Drood*?"

"Yep," Barbra said, holding up her copy. "I should have known Ivy's read it. It is a mystery, after all."

"It was pretty obvious," Boyd said. "It was Jasper."

Opal shook her head. "You can't prove it."

"Who else had a motive? There was one person, period. It was Edwin's uncle."

"What if Edwin wasn't even dead?" a woman Ivy didn't know asked.

"Then it wouldn't be a mystery, would it?" Opal asked.

"It would be. If he wasn't dead, he had to have been somewhere. That's still a mystery."

Barbra looked at me. "What do you think, Ivy?"

"I'm pretty sure he was dead. Charles Dickens's son said that he asked his father, and he confirmed it."

"Well, that's cheating," the woman said.

I smiled. "Sorry." I would keep the other things I'd studied about the book to myself.

"Who could it be besides Jasper?" Boyd asked. "I can't think of another person."

Opal took a cookie. "But the book wasn't finished. What if there were going to be other suspects? Have you ever seen a short Dickens novel? The man was paid by the word. I bet he was going to drag it out for five hundred pages."

"He wasn't paid by the word," Boyd said. "That was just a rumor."

"Then why did he use so many when fewer would have gotten the job done better?"

"Authors are odd. You find me one author who isn't, and I'll give you a dollar."

Opal rolled her eyes. "Let's get back on topic. Who could have killed Edwin besides Jasper?"

"What about Neville?" Barbra asked, pushing her purple hair behind her ear. "He had a huge fight with Edwin right before he died."

"Nah," said Boyd. "Jasper was in love with Edwin's gal. It was Jasper."

"What about the opium den woman?" someone said. "She was shady."

"Nope. Jasper all the way."

Opal glared at him. "I think I like it better when Boyd doesn't read the book."

Barbra nodded. "Boyd, you have to let other people express their opinions."

"Even if they're wrong?"

Barbra gave him a look, and he held up his hands in surrender. "Okay, okay."

"Does anyone else think it might have been Rose?" Opal asked.

Boyd threw his hands in the air. "Why would she kill him? She's not even a suspect!"

I smiled and shook my head.

"But they broke up."

"It was a mutual decision. They both wanted to move on. Why kill him?"

Opal shrugged. "I'm just saying. It's possible."

As amusing as the book club was, I had things to do. Jett texted me and said I could have my canopy and table back tomorrow, so I needed to make more cheesecake. I would have to move to another area, but I didn't want to be where Deputy Russell was killed anyway.

I went back to the kitchen and grabbed a mixing bowl.

"I have a few cheesecakes ready for you in the freezer," Carrie said from her place by the frying pan.

"You're a lifesaver," I said, plugging in the mixer.

"Do you know when José will be back?"

"No. I told him to watch Jett. I'm worried about him."

"I was surprised you came back."

Boyd came into the kitchen holding a cookie. "I can't handle Opal today. I think she likes to make stuff up about books and then argue with people."

I smiled. "I thought that was your job."

He chuckled. "Maybe that's why I don't like it when she does it. She's doing my job."

"Have you heard from José?"

"Yeah. He said it looks like the police are almost finished."

"I wish I'd never gone to the fair," I muttered, unwrapping a stick of butter. It was hard not to blame myself for Russell's murder. If Hanson was really behind it, he'd done it because of me.

Boyd patted me on the back. "Something would have happened whether you did or not."

"I don't know why Jett didn't run over and check out Hanson's alibi right when I told him about the cheesecake on his clothing."

"Deputy Ledford talked to him."

"How do you know?"

"Jett told me."

My mouth turned down. "Did he learn anything?"

"According to Ledford, Hanson bought a piece of cheesecake and dropped it on himself."

"I don't believe it," I said, grabbing the brown sugar. "Did you see anyone besides me selling cheesecake?"

"Nope."

"I didn't sell him any, so even if he was innocent of the murder, he still stole it. I know he took the display. That's why he got sick."

"I'm surprised you haven't searched his room more thoroughly."

"I was in a hurry."

Carrie turned from her cooking. "His friend came in today. He's still throwing up, so he'll probably stick to his room."

"Ledford should have pried more."

"I'm sure Jett will deal with it when he gets back. I'm going to get the animals from Brian. Call me if you need me."

I nodded and turned on the mixer. I didn't want to bake. Someone needed to check on Hanson and Brooke. Jett would get around to it, but what if they took off? Nothing was keeping them here.

"Do you want me to make those cookies for you?" Carrie asked. "You look like you'd rather be somewhere else."

"I can't leave you here without José. I'm fine."

The rest of the day dragged on as I made pan after pan of cookies. Carrie and Tiffany kept up with all the food orders, so all I had to do was bake. By the time the diner closed, I was ready to call it a night, but not until I checked on Jett.

Right as I was going to switch on the closed sign, Jett came in.

"Long day?" I asked, giving him a hug.

"Yep. Did you make enough cookies for tomorrow?"

"I think so. I might be short on cheesecake. Carrie made some, but I didn't feel like making any."

"I talked to Hanson."

I looked up at him. "Oh yeah?"

"I'm not sure what's going on with that guy. He's definitely up to something. I asked him if he saw anything suspicious, and he said he didn't want to talk about it. He wouldn't tell me where the cheesecake came from that was on his clothes either. That yells 'guilty' to me. Ledford took the clothing as evidence. He said he asked Hanson if he could, and he said yes, but now Hanson's mad he didn't get a warrant."

"I feel bad. I should have dealt with Hanson differently. I just don't know what I could have done to make him understand that I don't like him."

"You didn't do anything wrong. If he's guilty, it was all on him."

"Did you eat?"

"Breakfast."

"Come on, I just put away the enchiladas. I bet they're still warm." He followed me to the kitchen, and I pulled a container from the fridge.

"Is Hanson the only one you're looking at?"

"I'm looking into Brooke and Bill, and also the man who had the booth behind you. I don't think it was him, but I want to be thorough. It could have been a person who wasn't nearby most of the time, but I'm putting my money on Hanson."

I placed an enchilada on a plate and microwaved it for a few seconds, then handed it to him.

He sat at the island and took a bite. "Food sure tastes good after not eating for a while."

"I'm not excited to go back tomorrow."

"You made good money the first day."

"Yeah, but now I'll be nervous."

"Take José."

"He needs to be at the diner."

"Wednesdays aren't very busy, are they?"

I shook my head. "No, but with Anton gone, that puts a lot of stress on Carrie."

"Then take Boyd. He can hang out at the fair for hours without getting bored."

"Are you going to be there?"

"I don't think so. We've done all we can there, so now I need to question the suspects."

I tried not to look disappointed. "You're taking someone with you, right?"

He went to the fridge and took out the milk. "I'm not sure."

"Take one of the deputies."

He glanced at me as he poured milk into a glass. "You know, I used to take care of everything without any help?"

"But now you don't have to."

"I'll get Ledford to come with me."

"Promise?"

"Probably."

I glared at him. "That's not a good answer."

He grinned. "It's the type of answer you give me every time I try to get you to stay safe."

I sighed. He was right. "Whatever you do, be careful."

"I will. You be careful as well. Don't go anywhere alone."

After Jett finished eating and went home, I went up to my room and got ready for bed. If people didn't like to eat late, I would close the diner an hour earlier. I yawned and walked around looking for Creepers. I found him sitting in the window seat in my bedroom.

"Hello," I said, scooping him up. He meowed and put his paws on my shoulder. "Did you have fun with Brian today?"

It was a silly question. Brian spoiled all the animals he dealt with.

"Sorry I've been gone so much. Are you bored? I guess Boyd was playing with you earlier, and sometimes I think you like him more than me."

He batted at my hair, and I placed him on the bed.

"I would take you with me, but I wouldn't be able to control you at the fair, and you hate it outside."

Creepers ignored me and curled up on my comforter. I hurried through my nighttime routine and climbed into bed. I needed to get plenty of sleep to get through what would probably be a boring day tomorrow.

Chapter 8

I was surprised the following day when I got to my booth and saw it all set up with a new tablecloth. A new glass cake pedestal sparkled in the sun. Jett was definitely the best.

Boyd and I were busy for the first part of the day, and then, as more events began, the crowds died down. By evening, we were barely selling anything. Boyd left to go watch a pig race, and he came back with cotton candy that was as big as half of him.

"You're going to be sick," I said as he sat by me.

He grinned. "But happy. Do you want some?"

"No, thanks."

"You should go do something. Go on a ride or play some games."

I wrinkled my nose. "Fair games aren't my thing, and rides are only fun with someone."

"They have a haunted house."

"I'm definitely not going into a haunted house by myself."

"They have a Ferris wheel."

"I'm fine sitting here."

"Scared of Ferris wheels, huh?"

I smiled. "Maybe a little."

"You can burst into a murderer's house and wander all around, yet you're too scared to go on a Ferris wheel?"

"Yep. I've been on them a few times, but I hate them."

"You can't sit here all day. Go get a soda or something."

I tilted my head. "Are you trying to get rid of me?"

"No, I just think it's good to get up every now and then. At least take a lap around."

"Fine," I said, standing.

I walked around and bought a lemonade, then went over to talk to Bill.

"How are things going?" I asked.

"Alright," he said, leaning back on his chair legs. "I did a lot better when I was next to your booth. I didn't think you were coming back."

"I got my table back, so I figured I might as well. I don't want to lose all that booth fee money."

"Gotcha. I'm just glad no one's come by to interview me today. Yesterday, it felt like I couldn't get a break. Every lawman who was here thought they needed to talk to me separately. That could've been why my sales were down."

"That sounds frustrating."

"Yeah. It's like when you go to the doctor, and the nurse asks you a bunch of questions that you assume will be passed on to the doctor. Then the doctor comes in and asks the same questions."

I didn't know what to say to that.

"It looks like you've sold some chess sets."

"Four. That more than takes care of my booth fee. Any word on what happened to Russell? I keep thinking I'll hear something since the police aren't around today. Did they catch anyone?"

"Not that I know of."

"I should have paid more attention when I felt something near my feet. I just figured it was a dog or something, and I didn't want to lose a potential sale."

"Do you know anyone who didn't like Russell?"

"I don't know anyone who did. I'm a little nervous since I was so vocal about not liking him, and my booth was right next to you. That's probably why so many cops talked to me. I bet I'm at the top of the list of who killed him."

He watched me carefully like I might have some insight for him.

"Sheriff Malone tries to keep me out of that kind of thing."

He chuckled. "I've heard. You've solved a lot of murders since you came. You're going to make the law look bad at their jobs."

"No. Jett's good at his job. I've gotten lucky a few times."

"Are you trying to solve this one, then?"

I shrugged. "I'm pretty busy right now." I didn't want to lie, but I didn't want to advertise that I was going to try to figure it out.

"Not to make you paranoid or anything, but a person is standing down at the end of the row in a black hoodie. They haven't moved since you came over, and they're looking in your direction."

I frowned. "Are you sure they're looking at me?"

"Maybe not, but it looks like it. They're kinda far away."

"Which way?"

"To your left."

"I better go back to my booth. Thanks." I turned casually to my left and saw a figure in a black hoodie scurrying the other way. I could hurry and try to catch them, but I would have to run, and that would draw attention.

I speed walked to the corner where they had turned, but they had vanished. As I walked past the booths, I scanned all the people. No one around had a black hoodie. I normally wouldn't stress about it, but it was hot outside, so anyone wearing a hoodie was suspicious to me.

There wasn't a lot of reason for anyone to bother with me. I hadn't been actively working on the case. But if it was Hanson, that was another thing altogether. I returned to my booth and told Boyd.

"We better keep a close watch. It could have just been a person looking in your direction, though, so let's not get too nervous."

Just as he said it, something crashed into the glass cake stand, shattering it. I covered my mouth and let out a small shriek, and Boyd jumped to his feet.

"There!" he said, pointing. A figure in a dark hoodie was fleeing.

I jumped to my feet and tore off after them, weaving my way through the crowds. I hardly noticed the people I bumped into and kept my focus on the hoodie.

"Ivy!" José said, running up with me. "What are you doing?"

I didn't take time to wonder why José was here. "Follow that hoodie!" I said, pointing.

José chuckled under his breath and kept next to me.

The person ran into a large structure that said "Fun House" in rainbow bubble letters on the top.

"Great," I muttered, following them inside. José looked around. The first room was entirely pink. Big rose-colored trampolines on the side of the walkway were covered with bouncing teenagers. One of them jumped up and smashed into the wall, getting stuck.

"What?" I muttered.

"Velcro walls," José told me.

I nodded and moved across the room. No one had a hoodie. We went through a doorway, and I frowned. The floor in front of us was shuffling back and forth.

"Wait up!" Boyd said, running up next to us. Leaning over, he rested his hands on his knees and breathed hard.

"We have to hurry," I said. "Why don't you go back, Boyd? We've got this."

"I'm coming," he said.

I stepped onto the moving planks and almost lost my balance. I held my arms to the sides to try to stay steady. José ran past me, shifting from side to side, but he didn't fall. He jumped to the stable ground in front and turned back to us.

He grinned. "Faster might be easier."

I wasn't sure I could go any faster. I took slow, careful steps. Boyd scurried past me and joined José.

"Seriously?" I muttered. "José, go find the person in the black hoodie. They threw something at my table and were watching me earlier."

José's smile fell, and he turned and took off through a red-and-white-striped spinning tunnel. He went through it like he was walking on solid ground.

"I'm gonna call Jett," Boyd said, pulling out his phone.

I took a cautious step and rolled my eyes as three teenagers rushed past me. Taking a deep breath, I hurried forward and made it across the moving planks.

"I don't have any reception in here," he said.

I nodded. "Let's keep moving."

Looking at the rotating cylinders in front of me made me dizzy, but I needed to catch up to José. I ran through the spinning tunnel just like José had. I was glad he'd gone first so I could copy him. I probably would have gone slower if he hadn't sped through.

Turning back, I looked at Boyd.

He took a deep breath, stepped into the tunnel, moved upward, and fell. He kept moving up and down the cylinder wall and sliding back down. Before I could decide what to do, he got on his hands and knees and scurried through the tunnel faster than I would ever imagine he could go. When he got to me, he sat on the floor and panted.

"I'm getting too old for this type of thing."

"Are you alright?" I asked, offering my hand. He took it, and I pulled him to his feet.

"Fine. Maybe a few bruises."

I looked forward and blew out a breath. A mirror maze stood before us. "How do they build something like this to use for one week?"

"I'm sure they're experts at it. They move around from place to place, so they have to be good at setting it up and taking it down."

"We need to hurry. The person could already be out by now." We rushed into the maze, and after a few turns, I was almost sure we were never getting out. It all looked the same, and I didn't appreciate seeing myself in the mirror at every turn.

"There has to be a system," I said, looking over my shoulder. Boyd was gone. "Boyd?" Nothing. "Boyd?" I said louder.

"Over here!" his voice called. "I lost you somewhere."

I tried moving to where his voice was coming from but couldn't see him. "Where are you?"

"We're wasting time," he said. "Go without me, and I'll find you later."

I sighed and began moving as fast as I could.

"Boo!" a clown said, jumping out from behind a corner.

I yelled and slapped him on the side of the head.

"Ouch!"

I covered my mouth with my hands. "I'm so sorry. I didn't expect that."

"It's alright," he said, straightening his red wig. "I'm not supposed to jump out, so I guess I deserved it."

"Have you seen someone in a black hoodie come through?"

"Yeah, they're still in the mirrors."

"Thanks," I said, hurrying away. I looked over my shoulder. "If you find my booth, I'll give you a free cheesecake."

The clown gave me a thumbs-up. It was the least I could do after smacking him.

A loud crash made me stop and cringe, followed by a second crash and the sound of shattering glass. I made my way forward and turned a corner. José was sitting on the floor next to some broken mirrors.

"José!" I said, helping him to his feet. "What happened?"

He kicked at the glass. "I saw the person and charged at them. It was only their reflection, and I crashed into the mirror. I can't believe I was tricked like that."

Footsteps ahead made me take off running. José was with me. We were going to get banned from the fair any second. We ran out of the mirrors and into a room with a large tunnel that was only about three feet high.

I dropped to my knees and looked in. Someone was ahead, crawling quickly. I crawled after them, figuring José would follow. When I got to the end, I jumped out, and a puff of air blew into my face, causing me to jump. Two doors stood in front of me, swinging open and closed. José stood beside me and grabbed my arm.

"Ready? Go!" He pulled me through the doors and into a white room. The lights were blinking on and off, making everything appear unstable. The walls looked like they were moving in, but that was probably an illusion. No one appeared to be here.

I frowned. "Where did they go? They couldn't get through here that fast."

I looked around, but with the flickering lights, it was hard to focus. I couldn't make out any shapes.

"Run!" José said as the walls got closer. A scene from *Star Wars* flashed through my mind. I knew we weren't actually in danger, but my heart pounded as we ran through the room. The walls never hit us, and when we got out, the floor was stable. I took a deep breath.

"I shouldn't have left Boyd."

"He'll figure it out. Come on." We walked down a dark hallway and outside. I scanned the area but didn't see our person. A young man with a badge stood near the exit.

"Did a person in a hoodie come out?"

The man's brows came together. "Not that I remember."

I glanced at José. "That means he's still inside."

José turned to the man. "We need to see the person in charge."

"He'll be here in a minute. Someone just made a call on the walkie-talkie and said someone broke something inside."

"That was me," José said. "I ran into a mirror, and it shattered."

"Dang," the boy said. "You must have hit it hard. People crash into those all the time, and I've never heard of one breaking."

A man in a button-up plaid shirt holding a walkie-talkie approached them. "Hey, Kennith," he said to the man we were talking to. "Don't let anyone leave who comes out without questioning them."

"I broke the mirror," José said.

The man turned, and his eyebrow rose. He'd probably expected a teenager, not a fifty-year-old man in a polo shirt.

"One of my workers said they thought it was a person in a black hoodie."

"We were chasing that person," I said. "I'm a vendor, and they threw something at my display and broke it."

The man's walkie-talkie made static sounds, and someone said, "Hey, the person in the hoodie just ran out the entrance and disappeared into the crowd."

"Great," I muttered.

"I'll pay for the mirror," José said.

The man shook his head. "Don't worry about it. We have insurance."

"Our friend might be stuck inside," I said. "He was having trouble getting through."

"What does he look like?" Kennith asked. "I can go through. I know this place like the back of my hand."

"He's about seventy, bald, with a goatee."

Kennith raised his brow. "Seventy? I don't see people like that in here."

"Shut it down," the boss called. "We don't need anyone getting hurt. Where's Perry?"

"He passed by about twenty minutes ago, so he should be by any minute."

"When he comes by, tell him to go after the person in the hoodie."

I didn't want to put Perry down. He seemed like a nice guy, but if someone was running, he would never catch them. It would take time to get Jett here, and he was busy and might not be able to come anyway. One of the deputies was here somewhere, but I hadn't noticed them and didn't know how to contact them anyway.

Kennith went back into the fun house to look for Boyd.

"Should we wait for Boyd, or go look for the hoodie person?" I asked José.

"Wait. That person is long gone. They probably ran straight for the exit or ditched the hoodie. Looking for them would be a waste of time."

Chapter 9

"I can't believe they broke the new cake stand I got you," Jett said, sitting back in my recliner. "I'm not sure you should go back for the other days."

"They threw a rock at it," José said from the sofa. "I can't believe they hit it. I guess they might have been aiming at Ivy and missed."

Boyd sat next to him, eating a sandwich. "Don't make Ivy paranoid."

I sat on the armrest of the recliner and looked at Jett. "Of everything I told you, you only focus on the cake stand? José smashed two full-length mirrors, and I smacked a clown. And Boyd got stuck in the funhouse. They might have to put an age limit, so something like that doesn't happen again."

Boyd chuckled. "The fair gave me a coupon for a free meal."

Jett smiled. "It sounds like you had an eventful day. Could you tell if the person was a man or a woman?"

"No," I said. "I only ever saw the back of them."

"They were wearing white Adidas with blue stripes," José said. "I did manage to see that."

I rubbed my arm. "I bet it was Hanson."

"Nope," Jett said. "I was talking to him when this all happened."

I frowned. "Really? I was almost positive he killed Russell."

"He might have. It could have been a different person. I find it strange that the murderer would come back to break your cake stand. What would the point be?"

"Why would anyone do it?" Boyd asked. "It's not like we're in a competition or anything. I don't see any reason."

"Whoever killed Russell shouldn't have anything against me. I wasn't connected to him," I said.

"Yeah, but if they thought they were killing Jett, it could involve you," José said. "This could all be focused on you, but that made more sense if it was Hanson."

"Have you checked Russell's place?" I asked Jett.

"No. I'm not sure that would be useful. He wasn't killed there, and if the murder got the wrong person, it doesn't seem relevant."

I nodded even though I didn't agree.

Jett sighed. "I know you, Ivs. As soon as I leave, you're going to break into Russell's apartment and snoop."

I grinned. "You're crazy."

"I'm right. Don't go to his apartment."

"Why? He's not there. I don't see a reason for anyone to go inside."

"Exactly, so don't."

"I'm tired," I said. "It's been a crazy day." With luck, I could get Jett's mind off Russell's apartment. I was going as soon as I got a chance.

"I think my entire body is bruised," Boyd said. "I think I've hurt myself more since Ivy moved to Muddy Creek than in the last fifty years."

My mouth turned down. "You shouldn't follow me."

"I'm not complaining. My life's been much less boring, and I always have something to discuss before book club. I hope Zumba's cancelled tomorrow because I'm sore."

"No Zumba," I said. "I already canceled it for the fair, remember?"

"Right."

"Well, I'm going to bed," José said, standing. "I need to open the diner tomorrow morning."

"I just hope I can move to get up in the morning." Boyd laughed. "I'm going to be stiff." José helped him stand.

"I'll see you all tomorrow," I said, stifling a yawn.

"You coming?" José asked Jett.

"In a minute."

Boyd grinned. "Don't you know he has to kiss Ivy good night?"

I tilted my head and gave Boyd my best glare.

"I'll drop Boyd at home on my way," José said. They left and shut the door.

"I wish I'd seen Boyd in the funhouse," Jett said, pulling me onto his lap.

I put my arm around his neck. "He did the first part better than I did, but it went downhill after that. I still feel bad about hitting the clown."

He laughed. "Just be glad he didn't press charges."

"I am."

"I'm going to ask if they have cameras inside. If they do, we might be able to figure out who the person you were chasing was, and I could be entertained by watching the rest of you."

I groaned. "I hope they don't. José was the only one who went through smoothly."

He kissed my cheek. "I better go. Boyd gets worried if I'm not home at night. I don't know how he lived on his own for so long."

I jumped up. "Boyd's the best. It would have been boring today without him."

Jett stood and put his arms around me. "Go to bed after I leave."

I grinned mischievously. "What else would I do?"

He raised his eyebrow. "I don't even want to know. I might put a tracker on you so you can't get into trouble."

"What makes you think that would change anything?"

He leaned down and kissed me. "At least I would know you were on the move."

I waited fifteen minutes after he left before putting my shoes back on. I wouldn't put it past Jett to stand outside for a few minutes to make sure I didn't leave.

After ensuring Creepers was happy for the night, I grabbed my keys and peeked out the window. No sign of Jett. I went out and around to my gray Kia Soul and climbed in. I'd already asked José where Deputy Russell lived. He'd had a basement apartment near the edge of town.

I parked a ways down the street so the people who lived on the top floors of the house wouldn't be alerted. All the lights were out, and no cars were in the driveway. It was possible no one lived upstairs. I pulled on some gloves, which always made me feel a little like a criminal.

I crept around the house and walked down a few concrete steps. I tried the door and wasn't surprised to find it locked. A window well next to the door caught my attention. I climbed into it and tried to push the window open. It wasn't very deep, but I was sure it was full of bugs. I tried not to think about it.

The window shifted slightly, and I smiled. It wasn't locked, but it wasn't moving easily. Once I could get my fingers in, I pushed it the rest of the way. I jumped, though, and tried to see in the dark room. After grabbing my flashlight, I flipped it on and looked for a light switch. I figured seeing a light on would look less suspicious than seeing a flashlight bouncing around.

I flipped on the light and scanned the sitting room. It had an old flowery sofa and a beanbag. The TV mounted on the wall was one of the biggest I'd ever seen. I yawned and forced myself to look around. I should have gone to bed and come in the morning. I was going to be so tired tomorrow.

The room was small and didn't have a lot in it, so I walked around the rest of the house. My nose wrinkled when I went into the kitchen. It smelled like ramen and fish. For being the only person who lived here, Russell was messy. He had two sinks full of dishes, and none of the surfaces were clean. From the look of the carpet, the man hadn't owned a vacuum.

I scanned the cupboards, and my eyes darted back to one set that was zip-tied together. That was odd. A zip tie wouldn't keep a thief out. I pulled out the pocket knife Boyd gave me for my birthday. It wouldn't keep me out either. I quickly broke the tie and opened the cupboards.

My eyes went wide. It was full of money. Piles and piles of bills were held together in clumps with a band around them. I picked up a stack and flipped through them. They were all tens. If all the bills were tens, then a lot of money had been stashed here. I looked at another stack, and they were ones.

Now the question was, why? I couldn't think of any legitimate reason to keep this much cash. Something shady was going on. I stared at the money and wondered what I should do. Calling Jett was probably the best thing, but he was tired and might be annoyed I'd come when he told me not to.

A noise in the other room made me pause. It was the window being pushed open. I frowned and stuck the money back in the cupboard, then flipped off the kitchen light. I quickly opened the pantry door and got inside, closing it behind me.

My heart pounded as I listened. Light shone under the door, and I held my breath. This was the most obvious place to hide, but they probably weren't looking for me. They must be looking for the money. I wanted to peek out, but I forced myself to stay still.

I swallowed as slow footsteps walked across the tile floor. It felt like they were deliberately walking slowly to make my heart go crazy. The pantry smelled worse than the rest of the kitchen, and my shoe made a funny sound when I stepped back. I was probably standing in sticky syrup or something similar.

"Ivy?" Deputy Ledford said. I let out an annoyed breath. "Ivy? I know you're here. I saw your car."

I opened the door and came out, trying to look innocent. My shoe made a sticky sound with every step.

Deputy Ledford frowned and put his hands on his hips. "You aren't allowed to break into people's houses." It was hard to feel intimidated by him. He was only as tall as me, and he looked more tired than angry.

I shrugged. "I didn't break in. The window wasn't locked."

"You know what I mean."

"You gave me a heart attack."

His lips twitched up slightly. "I hope so. You're going to get in trouble one day."

"Why are you here?" I asked.

He raised his brows. "Why am I here? Why are you here?"

"Just looking around."

"And?"

"And what? That's all."

"Did you find anything?"

"Yep."

He rubbed his mustache. "What?"

I hid a smile. Ledford had never liked me, and I didn't mind keeping him in suspense. Our relationship had improved, but we were nowhere near friends.

"Look in that cupboard," I told him.

Ledford's boots clinked against the tiles as he went to the cupboard. He opened it and whistled. "That's a lot of money."

"Should I call Jett?"

"No. I'm on call right now. Sheriff Malone called me and asked me to drive by to make sure you weren't here."

"He called you?" I asked. Jett was definitely in trouble. He knew what my relationship with Ledford was like.

"I can't believe he doesn't trust me."

Ledford laughed. It was strange coming from him. I wasn't sure if I'd ever heard him laugh like that before. "Should he? You're always doing something you shouldn't."

"And you should be glad about that," I said, hoping he remembered the time I'd saved him.

He just grunted. "I'm going to search the rest of the house."

"Do you want help?"

He let out a long, slow sigh. "I suppose since you're going to do it anyway." He began opening all the cupboards.

"I looked in the cupboards with the money because they were zip-tied shut."

He snorted. "That sounds like Russell. I don't know how he made it through the academy. You look in all the cupboards, and I'll check his room."

It didn't take long to look through everything. Nothing appeared out of the ordinary.

Ledford came out. "He has drugs in his nightstand."

"Do you think he was dealing? Is that why he has so much money?"

"Perhaps. There isn't a lot, so I assume it's his own personal supply."

"Does anyone live upstairs?"

"No. It's been vacant for over a year, from what I've heard."

"Should we check? He might have stashed things."

"I'll talk to Sheriff Malone about it in the morning."

I frowned.

He gave me a half smile. "I go through the proper channels, unlike some people."

I wouldn't swear to it, but I was beginning to think I was growing on Ledford. He didn't sound half as annoyed as he usually did when I talked to him.

"I'm going to leave then," I said.

Ledford gave me a sharp glance. "Don't come back. I'm going to keep looking around, and I'll drive by several more times tonight to make sure you aren't here."

I nodded and went out the door. I walked through the night air and over to my car. I wasn't going to sleep tonight, trying to figure out what Russell had been up to. This might mean whoever killed him had meant to kill him, and not Jett. That didn't make sense if you added the person in the black hoodie. If this was all about Russell, why bother me?

Chapter 10

I stood outside Jett's house the next day so I could talk to him before he talked to Ledford. Of course, Ledford could have called or texted him, but from what I'd seen, Ledford liked to tell on me to Jett's face to see his reaction.

Jett came out, and Conan followed him. I smiled as Jett tried to get him inside. Every time he tried to shut the door, the puppy would squeeze back out. Boyd eventually came and grabbed Conan, and Jett shut the door.

"Is it like that every day?" I asked.

Jett grinned. "Only on the days I can't sneak past him." He kissed me quickly. "What's up?"

"You sent Ledford after me."

His smile grew. "I knew you would go there."

"Well, Ledford was too slow. I was already inside."

"Did he kick you out?"

"No. He joined me."

"Sure he did."

"He did. We found a bunch of money and some drugs."

Jett laughed. "Very funny. You didn't find anything, did you?"

"I'm not joking."

His smile fell. "Really?"

"Yep. There's a cupboard full of money and drugs in the nightstand."

"Dang. I should have checked."

We walked over to his truck. "I'm sure Ledford's at the office dying to tell you all about it."

"I bet. Are you going to the fair?"

"No. I made up more than the week's fees, and the new spot they placed me in isn't that great."

"Good. I don't want you there with someone dangerous after you."

"I'm not sure anyone's after me. It could have been a prank. Now that we found the stuff at Russell's apartment, I'm not as convinced it was someone after you."

"I wouldn't be surprised." Jett pulled out his phone and glanced at a text. "Ledford wants to meet me at Russell's place. I'll see you later."

He got in his truck and drove away. I watched him go, then got in my car. I couldn't decide what to do. The diner wouldn't need me today with José there, but I couldn't think of anything better to do. I should talk to Hanson or Brooke, but I didn't want to.

The door to the house opened, and Boyd came out holding Conan. He walked over to my car, so I rolled down the window.

"Jett forgot to give Conan his medicine," he said. "I can't get him to take it, and he needs to have it in the morning."

"I can take him over and have Jett give it to him."

"Let me go grab it."

He passed Conan through the window, and he cuddled against me.

"You're such a good boy," I said, petting his back.

A few minutes later, Boyd came out with the pet carrier and a bottle. We put Conan inside, and I drove over to Russell's house. Jett's truck and Ledford's car were outside. I took Conan out of the carrier and walked around to the back. The door was unlocked, so I went in.

I found Jett and Ledford in the kitchen. They both turned when I entered. Both of them were frowning.

"You didn't give Conan his medicine," I said.

Jett came over and took the medicine from my hand and quickly gave it to him.

I glanced at the open cupboard. "You cleared out the money?"

"No, it's gone," Ledford said.

"Gone? We were just here last night."

"And I drove past every hour and never saw anything."

Conan barked, and I placed him on the floor.

"Don't blame yourself," Jett told Ledford. "Now we need to figure out who cleaned it out and who killed him. My guess is that it's the same person, but who really knows?"

"Are the drugs gone?"

"No," Jett said. "We've got them. Nothing else seems to be disturbed."

"I'll take Conan home."

Jett nodded.

"Conan!" I called, when I didn't see him. "Come on, boy!"

He came walking back into the kitchen with a hand-sized notebook in his mouth. I kneeled down and gently took it away.

"What's this?" I asked, opening it. There was a list of names of people from the town, with an amount written next to them. I handed it to Jett.

"Interesting," he said, showing it to Ledford. "I think more has been going on with Deputy Russell than we ever would have imagined."

"Looks like it," said Ledford. "This might explain where all the money came from."

"But not why."

"A lot of these people have had trouble with the law before."

Jett turned the page, then the next one. "It looks like he has a page for every town in the county."

"Do you think it's drug related?"

"Possibly."

"I would think if it was, there would be more drugs here."

"Maybe he sold them all?"

"I guess that's possible."

I picked up Conan. "Good boy. You might make a good police dog after all. Boyd's going to take credit, you know."

Jett laughed. "He will."

I took Conan back to Boyd.

"Guess what?" I asked as I handed Conan to Boyd at the front door. "Conan found a clue."

Boyd's eyes lit up. "What kind of clue?"

"He found a notebook with a list of names and dollar amounts. One of them might be the killer."

Boyd rubbed Conan's head. "I knew he had it in him. Who says a Maltese can't be a police dog?"

Conan licked Boyd and wiggled until he put him down.

"What's next?" Boyd asked.

"I don't know. If one of the people in the notebook is the killer, then it wasn't Hanson. I'm still not ready to let that go. He was covered in cheesecake and blueberries. Also, if someone was only after Russell, what's with the person in the hoodie? I have so many questions that are still unanswered."

"Did you see who any of the people in the notebook were?"

I frowned. "I did, but all I remember thinking was that they were from town. I only read the first few. One might have been Fran Escolson."

"There's no way Fran's into something illegal," Boyd said. "She went to school with me. Nice gal."

My lip quirked up. Fran was about seventy. She came to book club and occasionally, Zumba. I'd talked to her a few times but never about anything important.

"I'll talk to her," I decided. "She might at least be able to tell me why her name was in the book. I'm wondering if it's some type of drug deal."

"Nah," Boyd scoffed. "There's no way Fran is into that type of thing. She's a health nut. She actually reads labels on food and doesn't eat them if they have things she doesn't agree with. Fran gets angry if anyone ever brings up red dye. I do it every once in a while just for fun."

I grinned. "You need more hobbies."

He chuckled. "It's possible."

"Do you want to go talk to her?"

"Sure."

We made the drive out to Fran's farm. It was only a mile outside town and not very big. Boyd said she sold off most of the land when her husband died and just kept the house and a small yard and garden. The gray house was a neat two-level structure with big windows and shutters.

"How do we bring this up?" I asked.

Boyd shrugged. "Just ask. She might not mind."

We got out of the car and walked up to the house. I rang the bell and waited. The door opened, and Fran peeked around the corner.

"Boyd, Ivy! Come in." She pulled open the door and let us enter. She led us to a small sitting room and had us sit on an overstuffed couch. She sat on a rocking chair. "What brings you two around?"

I took a deep breath. "Did you hear about Deputy Russell?"

Fran's smile faded, and her brow wrinkled. "What about him?"

"He's dead," Boyd said.

Fran's frown became less pronounced. "That's too bad. What happened?"

"He was murdered."

"Murdered? Mercy. Who did it?"

I shook my head. "We don't know yet."

She twisted the end of her gray braid. "Why are you telling me?"

I decided to pretend we knew more than we did and hoped Boyd didn't give me away. "There was a book found in Deputy Russell's things. He wrote some things in it. Some were about you."

Fran's lips came together, and she growled. "I hate that man."

"We want to help you."

"I suppose he had the pictures in the notebook? I don't see why it's all such a big deal. All I do with the coca leaves is make tea."

I didn't know what coca leaves were. Chocolate maybe? That was my best guess.

"It's only illegal because people can get cocaine from it. I would never use my plants for that."

Ah.

"The tea isn't illegal?"

"It is in the United States. I only use it for medicinal purposes. I had to grow my own plants because it's impossible to get legally."

"I never took you as someone to do anything illegal," Boyd said.

Fran sighed. "I went down to Colombia to visit my nephew. We had the tea every morning. It makes me feel better. My health isn't great, you know. I try to eat healthy and exercise, but sometimes I need something else."

"And that's why Deputy Russell was blackmailing you?" I asked.

"I wouldn't say blackmailing. I just paid him a little every month to keep it quiet."

Boyd leaned forward. "That's called blackmail, Fran."

She covered her eyes with one hand. "I know."

"Can we see the plants?" I asked.

"I suppose. I guess I'm going to jail, anyway." She stood, and we followed her down a set of stairs to a dark basement. I wanted to tell her she probably wouldn't go to jail, but I didn't know anything about things like this.

"Wow," I said when she flipped on a light. The basement was humid, and lights shone onto large raised garden beds. Plants were thriving down here, but I didn't recognize any of them.

"Right here," she said, pointing at a container with three-foot-tall plants. They were bright green with oval leaves. Small yellowish-white flowers grew in clusters.

"You must be good at growing things," I said.

"I grew up on a farm."

"How much were you paying Deputy Russell?"

"A hundred a month."

Boyd scratched his head. "How did he know you had this? He would have had to snoop."

"I'm assuming someone told him. I used to make the tea for a few people around town. When the deputy confronted me, he told me I could pay less if I told him about anything illegal in town he might not know about. I didn't know anything, but I assume that's how he was getting information. He also asked me for some seeds."

"Why would he want seeds?"

She shrugged. "I suppose he wanted some for himself."

"Do you still make the tea?" I asked.

"I do, but I don't give it to anyone. Not when someone is a squealer, and I have to pay the deputy every month whether I make it or not. So am I arrested?"

"We aren't the law. I'm not sure what will happen."

"I guess the sheriff has the notebook?"

I nodded.

She sighed. "I figured it would get out, eventually. Everything does."

Chapter 11

"This smells so good," Jett said, sitting at my small kitchen table.

I smiled. "And it isn't dessert." Almost everything I do in the kitchen is a dessert, but I'd found this recipe and decided to try it.

He scooped some up with his fork and twirled it to catch the stringy cheese. "What is it?"

"Loaded potato and chicken casserole."

"That's a lot of bacon on top." He took a bite. I hadn't tried it yet, so I wasn't sure how it would taste. "That is the best thing I've ever eaten."

I grinned and sat down. I put some on my own plate and took a bite. I closed my eyes. This was something I could eat until I got a stomachache. There was no way I was kissing Jett when he left. My breath was going to be horrid from the garlic.

"You should put this on the menu."

"It's too much work. We can't spend two hours on things that might not get ordered, and I bet it's not as good microwaved."

"Probably not. So what's with the food?"

I took a sip of water. "What do you mean?"

"I figure you're trying to make me happy before you tell me you stumbled in on a crime boss or something."

"Nothing like that. I just wanted to try it."

"Well, it's a winner."

"I did find something out, but it's not a huge thing."

"I knew there was something."

I grinned. He knew me too well. "I talked to Fran. She was paying Deputy Russell every month so he wouldn't arrest her for growing coca plants."

Jett wiped his mouth with a napkin and frowned. "Fran? That's odd. I wouldn't have expected that. I bet she makes tea."

"Yes." I was a little disappointed. I didn't think Jett would know what coca plants were. I guess that was silly since it's his job to know about those things.

"I figured the lists were either for blackmail or drugs. I talked to a few people on the list, but they weren't talking. They all claimed they didn't know what the list or money was all about. I guess I should talk to Fran."

I took another bite as I thought.

"This is seriously so good. I might not even mind microwaved leftovers."

"I'll give you some." I smiled mischievously. "What are the chances you'll give me a list of the people in the notebook?"

He smiled and winked at me. "No chance."

"Dang it. I should have memorized it before I handed it over."

"Too late. And you won't ever find it."

I frowned. "You hid it from me?"

"Not from you personally, but it's with evidence."

I blew out a breath. "Can you just tell me some of the people?"

"Nope."

"I'll ask Ledford."

Jett burst out laughing. "You think he'll tell you?"

"Maybe. I wouldn't say we're friends or anything, but he's warming up to me."

"He wouldn't let you see any evidence."

"I bet Jane would."

A flash of uncertainty crossed Jett's face, then he smiled. "She can't get into the evidence."

Someone knocked on the door.

"I'll be back," I said, walking into the living room and to the door. I opened it to see Bill. His sandy-blond hair hung to his shoulders, and he gave me a small smile.

"Hi, Ivy. Can I talk to you for a minute?"

"Yes, come in."

He stepped inside, and I closed the door. Jett came walking out, and Bill groaned. "I guess it's better to talk to both of you, but I was hoping Ivy could smooth it over for me. It smells good in here."

"Come eat," I said.

"I can't impose."

"We have plenty." He followed us into the kitchen, and I handed him a plate. We all sat down and ate quietly for a few minutes.

"This is one of the best things I've eaten in a while."

"Thanks."

He kept his eyes on his plate. Jett shot me a questioning look, and I shrugged. I couldn't imagine what he wanted to say. I didn't know him well, and he looked guilty.

When he finished, he sat back and sighed. "I haven't been paying my sales tax."

Jett leaned forward and rested his elbows on the table. "What do you mean?"

"I sell my things at events. I know you're supposed to file and pay the sales tax, but I never do. I mean, I pay a little, but it's kind of an honor system, and I only pay enough not to look suspicious."

My eyebrows came together. "Why would you tell me?"

"Deputy Russell found out. He was blackmailing me. Now that he's been killed, I'm sure he has records somewhere, and I'm going to end up in trouble. I wanted to tell now and deal with my consequences."

Jett's mouth turned down. "You're only coming forward because you knew you were going to get caught."

He shrugged. "Pretty much. I'm trying to be honest."

Jet nodded. "How much were you paying him?"

"Two hundred a month."

"How much did you owe in sales tax?"

"I don't keep track. Probably about a thousand a year."

"So you were paying Deputy Russell more than you would've had to pay in a year?"

"Yes. I had to, though, or I would have been in more trouble."

"Why tell me?" I said, still confused.

"I didn't want to tell Sheriff Malone, and I know you've solved a bunch of things in town. I figure you were likely to find the incriminating evidence."

Jett didn't look happy to hear that. I probably should stay out of his job. If I were him, I would be annoyed with me.

"I also worried you might think I was the one who killed Deputy Russell in your booth. I don't want any hard feelings, so I thought I better come clean."

"It doesn't look good," Jett said. "You have a motive, and you were close."

Bill frowned and looked at his empty plate. "I know."

"You were on my list before you came," Jett said. "I appreciate you coming forward before I had to come to you. I'll let you know if there's anything else I need."

Bill nodded and stood.

"Please don't leave town until this is all cleared."

"Alright." He looked at me. "Thanks for dinner."

I nodded, and he left.

"What do you think about that?" Jett asked me.

"I don't know. He looks sorry."

Jett raised his eyebrow. "Sorry? He looked scared to get in trouble. I'm not sure he's sorry as much as he's sorry he's caught."

"You think he killed Deputy Russell?"

"No. I just think he's sad he can't go on breaking the law and evading taxes."

"I'm surprised Deputy Russell found so many people to blackmail."

Jett scooped more food onto his plate. "I'm going to have heartburn, but it will be worth it."

I smiled. It might be time to start learning to cook as well as bake. "How many people were in his notebook?"

"Thirty-five."

"Wow. So you have to talk to all of them?"

"Yep. I need to figure out who was at the fair and why they were paying Russell."

"That should narrow it down. How many people would be at the fair?"

"You'd be surprised. There isn't a lot to do around here."

"Have you talked to Brooke?"

"For a few minutes."

"I wish they hadn't come. I still think it was probably Hanson."

"He's up high on my list. He isn't giving me a good alibi, and he won't tell me why he was covered in cheesecake. Did I tell you his prints were on Bill's table leg? He was definitely the one who crawled under the tables and made the mess."

"Then why haven't you arrested him?"

"Being under the table doesn't make him a murderer. Just suspicious."

"I'm going to talk to him tomorrow."

A shadow crossed Jett's face. "Make sure you're in public."

"I will. You look tired. You should go to bed."

He stood and picked up his plate. "I'll do the dishes first."

"I can get them."

"Nope. You spent two hours making that delicious food, so I'm going to clean your whole kitchen in hopes that you'll make it again someday."

"I'll make it again, even if you go home."

"You do a lot. I owe you."

"I'll help," I said, grabbing my plate. The dishes were piled higher than usual because making this casserole had taken a lot of prep and a lot of dishes.

Creepers came in and rubbed against my legs.

"Hungry?" I asked him.

"I've never been a cat person, but now that Conan's destroying my house, I'm beginning to wonder if I should be. Cats seem a lot less destructive."

"Conan's still a puppy. He'll mellow. I think." I'd never been around dogs much, so I wasn't speaking from experience. "Creepers is more passive than some cats, and he doesn't scratch everything up."

"Conan chews everything."

"He probably needs more outside time. How often do you walk him?"

"I take him out in the morning, and Boyd takes him in the afternoon. If I had time, I'd put in a fence so he could stay outside more, but that would take time I don't have, and I don't want to sink any more money into that house."

"You don't plan to stay there?"

"No."

I grinned and opened the dishwasher. "What about your tree?" Jett's mom had told me he only bought his house because of the large willow in the front yard.

He put a mixing bowl in the sink and turned on the water. "I've learned not to buy a house because of a tree.

I've put so much money into that place. Do you think you want to stay living above the diner long term?"

I put some cups in the dishwasher and avoided eye contact. "No. It's good for what I need now, but not forever."

We'd talked about marriage once, but it had been a while ago, and I didn't know what Jett was thinking about the whole thing. I also didn't know if he was the type to date for years before settling down. I wanted to ask, but that felt like it might be awkward.

Jett had joked about having three kids and a dog, but I didn't know if that was what he really wanted. It sounded good to me, but I didn't want to be pushy. Staying above the diner with kids and a dog would be too noisy for everyone involved.

"When will it not be good?"

I blinked. I'd gotten lost in my thoughts. "What?"

"When will you not want to live up here?"

I shrugged and kept loading. "It might be nice to have a yard someday and not to smell the diner every minute of my life."

"It's nice here, though."

"Yeah. It's good for now. That's why I'm a cat person. A dog would be terrible up here."

Jett's face fell. "You got me a dog."

"You like dogs."

Jett shut the dishwasher and took my hand. "Yeah, but what happens when we decide to—mesh our lives together?"

I let out a nervous giggle. "Mesh our lives together? What's that supposed to mean?"

He stepped closer, and my heart began thumping. I stepped back and bumped into the fridge. Jett stepped forward and pushed a strand of hair behind my ear. "I know, I'm not poetic. When we get married, we can't live in my old house with Boyd. That leaves this place, and Conan will tear it apart."

I turned my head sideways so I wouldn't be talking with my garlic breath in his face. "We could sell your house and rent out my apartment."

"Why aren't you looking at me?"

I turned and covered my mouth with one hand. "I have garlic breath."

He grinned. "So do I."

I smirked. "I know. I can smell it."

His grin widened. "If we both have garlic breath, we're even." He put his hand behind my head and leaned in and kissed me. I wrapped my arms around his neck and forgot about the garlic.

Chapter 12

"That cupcake is the best one you've ever done," Carrie said, examining my frosting flowers.

"I think I'm finally catching on."

"Once you get it, you don't even have to think about it. It's like riding a bike."

I laughed. "I won't tell you about the last time I rode a bike. It wasn't pretty." I thought back to the time I'd ridden Boyd's electric bike down a hill. I'd almost crashed.

Boyd poked his head into the kitchen. "Hey! Ivy," he loudly whispered. He pointed dramatically at the dining room. I peeked out the window, and my face fell. Brooke and Hanson were sitting at a booth. I wanted to talk to both of them, but not together.

I washed my hands and went out to greet them. "Hey, guys. Feeling better, Hanson?"

"Yeah. That was a nasty bug."

I raised my eyebrow. "Uh-huh."

"I guess it's going around," he said.

"Can I talk to you outside?"

Brooke rolled her eyes, and Hanson jumped up and followed me. I held open the door and waited for him to walk out.

"Hanson, I'm not stupid. I know you stole my cheesecake. There's not a stomach bug going around. You ate hot, old cheesecake."

"I don't know why you think it was me. You have no proof. What, you're going to try to send me to jail for a ten-dollar cheesecake?"

"I don't care about the cheesecake. You got what you deserved, and there is actually evidence that you were under the table. What I care about is finding out who killed Deputy Russell."

He held up his hands. "Whoa, whoa. Are you saying you think I killed him? I know I'm a suspect because I was around, but you can't believe it was me."

"I can't see any reason to be under the table if you're innocent."

He let out an annoyed breath. "I don't have to explain myself to you."

"No, you don't. Don't come into my diner ever again."

"You're banning me?"

A sly smile spread across my face. "I am."

"You can't do that."

"I can, actually."

Hanson ran a hand through his hair and looked up at the sky. "I went to your table, and you weren't there. I figured the day was over, and you didn't need the cheesecake. I grabbed a piece and ate it, okay?"

I folded my arms and drummed my fingers against them. "Then you thought, hmm, I think I'll crawl under the table? That makes perfect sense."

"I decided to take the entire cheesecake. It didn't taste bad. I regret that now of course. Someone was coming toward me, and I thought it was the sheriff, but it must have been the deputy. I knew he would be annoyed I had your cheesecake, so I dropped down and went under the table. I dropped most of the cheesecake. That's why it ended up all over my pants and under the table."

I stared at him, wondering how much to believe.

"If you were there, you must have heard something. That would have been really close to when the deputy was killed."

"I just wanted to get out of there. I crawled under the table next to yours and came out the side. I took off and came back to Muddy Creek. I swear that's what happened."

"When you crawled under the table, was someone sitting in the other booth?"

"No. I saw the guy who had been sitting there while I was hurrying to the exit. He was walking back."

My mouth turned down. Bill told me he felt something touch his leg around that time. Either Bill or Hanson was lying—unless a dog really had been under the table and touched Bill's leg like he thought. That could have happened before or after, I would have to ask.

"Did you see anyone else?"

"No. Everyone went to see the fireworks."

"I wonder why the deputy was at my booth."

"He was eating a cookie that I'm sure he didn't pay for."

"Where was Brooke?"

"When?"

"When you were stealing the cheesecake?"

"It's not like I was really stealing. We're still friends, right? It's more like sharing."

"You're delusional. Where was Brooke?"

"At the fireworks. When I got to the car, I texted her, and she came, and we went back to the B&B."

I nodded. "I'm going to talk to her."

He rubbed his chin. "I doubt that's a good idea. She doesn't like you."

"No kidding," I went back in the diner and sat in the booth across from Brooke. Hanson had the decency to stay outside.

"What do you want?" she asked.

"Where were you when Deputy Russell was killed?"

"Who are you, the police?"

"You can't answer?"

She glared. "I was watching the fireworks."

"For how long?"

"Only a few minutes. Then Hanson texted me and said we needed to go, so I left."

"Did you walk past my booth?"

"Yes."

"And you didn't see anything odd?"

"Nope. I wasn't looking, though."

"Was Hanson acting weird when you got to the car?"

She sighed and played with the wrapper from her straw. "He was annoyed because he ruined his pants. He kept muttering things. When Hanson's in a bad mood, I back off. We didn't talk on the drive."

"When you passed the booths, did you notice whether the person in the booth next to me was still there?"

She raked her fingers through her long black hair. "No. I told you. I wasn't paying attention."

"Did Hanson tell you the reason he was covered in cheesecake?"

She gave me an unfriendly glare. "I hope you aren't going to accuse him."

"How do you explain the cheesecake on his clothing?"

"I don't. We didn't talk about it. I figured he might tell me in the morning, but then he was throwing up."

"Hey, Ivs," Jett said, approaching the booth. "Can I talk to you for a minute?"

I gave Brooke a tight smile and went upstairs with Jett.

"What is it?" I asked after I closed the door to my bedroom.

"Brooke looked ready to take your head off. I think you should back off."

"She wasn't helpful anyway," I grumbled. My eyes lit up. "I think we can narrow things down to Bill or Hanson."

"Why is that?"

"Hanson said there wasn't anyone at Bill's table when he crawled under it. Bill said he felt someone touch his leg. That means one of them is lying."

Jett scratched his chin. "Or it could mean Hanson was in a panic and didn't notice Bill was still there."

I blew a frustrated breath of air upward, sending a strand of hair fluttering. "That could be true. Hanson said he saw Bill walking when he was leaving, though. Weren't there any prints on the stone cake stand?"

"Sure. Tons. That thing wasn't sanitary at all."

"People kept touching it. I think it's because it's so smooth."

"Bill's and Hanson's prints were on it, along with a bunch of random people."

I tilted my head and thought. "I saw Bill and Hanson touch it when I wasn't talking to them."

"Someone's looking at it to see if any of the prints would match the way someone would hold it as a weapon."

"They can figure that out?" I was impressed.

"Maybe. It depends on how they did it."

"What about the rock the person in the hoodie threw? Did it have prints?"

"I wasn't there, remember? No one kept the rock, so I never saw it."

I groaned. "I didn't even think about it until now. Were Brooke's prints on the stand?"

He put his hands on his hips and looked at the ceiling. "I can't remember. I can make a call."

"I don't think it was her. I just wondered."

"The rock couldn't have been Hanson. He was in Muddy Creek when it happened."

"Right." I'd forgotten about that.

"Tomorrow's the Fourth of July. I'm going to be at the fair all day, and I need to stay for the fireworks."

My mouth turned down. "I might come, but not to sell things. The diner closes early tomorrow. I wanted all my employees to have time for fireworks. I'm going back down to see if Brooke is still there."

Jett gave me a warning look. "Don't make her mad."

I smiled. "Me?"

We both went down to the dining area. Brooke was gone. I didn't really know what to say to her anyway. Jett had to go check on some things, so I went in the kitchen to help.

José turned from where he was mixing something in a bowl. "Have you checked Bill's house?"

I pointed at myself. "Me?"

He chuckled. "Don't try to look innocent. Who else around here would sneak into someone's house?"

"Boyd?" Carrie offered.

I smiled at her.

José shook his head. "He wouldn't do it without you leading him."

"I don't see the point," I said. "He already told us why he was paying Deputy Russell. Jett said he called and told the tax people about it and paid. They didn't even fine him for some reason."

I tapped my fingers against the island. "Dang it, José. Now I feel like I have to check out Bill's house."

José laughed. "He's at the fair. No one's around to see you."

"Are you coming with me?"

José looked at Carrie, and she rolled her eyes. "Go. We're fine here."

José nodded and finished what he was doing. I sent Boyd a text and told him what we were doing, just so multiple people would know where we were if we went missing.

Carrie shook her head at us. "If the two of you ever go to prison, it will be for something you've done while you were trying to solve a crime."

José grinned. "I'm sure that's right."

Chapter 13

"What does Bill do besides carving?" I asked as I pulled up to a neat white house. It wasn't huge, but it was fancy. Plantation shutters covered all the windows, and the roof and siding appeared new. I fiddled with my bracelet as I studied the area.

José unbuckled his seat belt. "I think that's all he does. He's passionate about it. He has an online store besides selling at events."

We got out of my car and stood looking at the house. One thing that made snooping nice in Muddy Creek was that most people didn't have close neighbors. I couldn't see any houses on the dirt road we'd come in on.

"Boyd," José said, pointing down the road.

I squinted. Sure enough, a bike was getting closer.

"I'm surprised he can ride that thing on the dirt."

"Electric bikes are nice," José said. We waited until Boyd reached us.

He got off the bike and grinned. "Bet you didn't expect to see me."

"We sure didn't," I said.

Boyd took a backpack off and pulled it around. Conan's head popped up, and he barked a happy bark.

"You brought Conan?" I exclaimed. "That's the last thing we need when we're trying not to draw attention."

"Who found Deputy Russell's notebook? It was this guy."

"We can't take a dog into someone's house. Especially an only slightly potty-trained dog."

"I'll keep him outside," he said, putting Conan on the ground. He clipped a leash to his collar. "We'll walk around the property and see if he finds anything."

"Alright, but don't get into anything."

José grinned. "Coming from Ivy, that sounds a bit hypocritical."

Boyd chuckled. "That's what I was thinking."

I gave them a small smile. "If I get myself into trouble, that's one thing. I don't want to get you guys into trouble."

"Do you think Jett will ever arrest you?" Boyd teased.

I shrugged. "If he had to, he would."

José pulled gloves from his pocket and put them on. I pulled out my own. We should put together kits and sell them to people. We could call them kits for people who didn't know how to mind their own business. That was definitely us.

I tried the door, and it was locked. Boyd disappeared around the back, and José and I tried all the windows. Bill kept his house locked up tight, and he had good locks. I had some things in my purse to pick a lock, but not the kind of locks Bill had.

Conan was yipping somewhere behind the house. José and I walked to the backyard. Boyd and Conan were standing by a shed.

"Conan wants to go in here," Boyd said. "There has to be something inside. I've been training him, you know."

We walked over to the shed, and José studied the lock.

"It's a good lock," he said. "Bill doesn't want people getting into his things."

I spotted a window on the side. "I might be able to see in the window." I walked over to the small window and peeked in. I couldn't make anything out. I pushed on the window, and it slid open. "I guess Bill missed something."

José stared at the small opening. "Do you think you can fit in there?"

I studied the window. "It will be tight."

"I'll boost you," José said, grabbing my legs and propelling me upward. I grabbed the window frame and pushed my head and shoulders through. With luck, my hips would make it. I would never live that down if I got stuck in the window. Thankfully, my hips made it past, and I turned myself so I could sit in the window with my legs hanging down on the outside and my head inside the dim shed.

"I'm not sure I can get in without falling back."

"Don't do that," Boyd said. "It's too high."

I pulled up one leg and put my foot on the window ledge, then the other so I was squatting on the window. I awkwardly put one leg behind myself and felt my gloves slip a little where I was gripping the sides.

"I wish I was recording this," Boyd said.

"Yeah," José said. "It's going to be hard to explain when we have to call for an ambulance."

I rolled my eyes and tried to shift my weight. "I won't need an ambulance." That was what I told myself, but it was a concern. I pulled my other leg inside and felt myself drop. My arm scraped against the window as I went down, but I landed on my feet.

"You alright?" José asked, peeking in the window.

"Fine," I said, ignoring the throbbing on my arm. I glanced around the shed. A long metal workbench was covered in wood shavings. It smelled like my seventh-grade woodshop class.

"Any drugs?" Boyd called in. "Conan's going crazy."

"Not so far." I pulled a small flashlight from my purse and shined it on the shelves. Light came from the window, but not enough to see any details.

Boyd poked his head through the window. "Should I come in?"

"No!" José and I said at the same time.

"I could be helpful."

"You won't fit," I said. "I barely made it."

"You never know unless you try."

I turned and wagged my finger at him. "If you get yourself wedged in the window so I can't get out, we'll have to call Jett, and that's not something I want to have to explain."

"Okay, okay." He chuckled.

A shelf above the workbench held carved animal statues. I picked up a monkey. It was rounded, almost like a cookie jar, and had incredible detail.

"Bill's talented," I said, turning it in my hands. I held it up by the window so they could see, and something shifted inside. "I think it opens." The monkey had a line going around its neck. I twisted it, and the head came off.

"What's inside?"

I swallowed. "A big wad of money."

José whistled. "Money hidden in a shed sounds suspicious."

"It really does." I put it down, then took out my camera and snapped a few pictures.

"Are there more?"

"Yes." I put the monkey's head back on and placed it back where I'd found it. I took a carved elephant and pulled it open. It was empty. The next two were full of money. I replaced them and shined my light under the bench. Taped-up packages were stacked on each other. I pulled one out. It had a name on it. I carefully pulled off the packing tape, doing my best not to rip up the box.

"What are you doing in there?" José asked.

"Hold on." I opened the box and found another monkey statue. Pulling off the head, I frowned. I stuck my hand inside and pulled out a handful of brown seeds. My phone rang, and I jumped, dropping some of the seeds. I grabbed them and stuffed them back into the monkey.

"Hello?" I said, taking Jett's call.

"Hey, Ivs. Remember how we shared our location with each other?"

My eyes narrowed. "What are you talking about?" I put the monkey back in the box and closed it. I grabbed a roll of packing tape from the bench.

Jett sighed. "I can see where you are on my phone."

I frowned. "Oh, right."

"So where are you?"

I smiled. "Shouldn't you know?"

"According to my phone, you're at Bill's house."

"Why would I be at Bill's house?"

He chuckled softly. "With you, who knows? I wouldn't be shocked if you were on his roof trying to go down his chimney."

"Ha-ha. If it makes you feel better, I'm nowhere near being in his house."

"Then what are you doing? Did I just hear Conan?"

I looked up at the window. Boyd was showing Conan inside the shed. I glared at him, and he grinned.

"Can I call you back later? I'm trying to—do something."

"I'm sure you are. Is Boyd with you?"

"Yep. And José."

"Alright, but when I get home, my dog better be there."

"Take that up with Boyd."

"I will."

"Love you." I hung up, not giving him a chance to ask anything else.

I tried to tear off a piece of tape, but it got caught on my glove, and I had to start over. Once I had the package back to the way I found it, I stood. "Oh no. I forgot to take a picture of the seeds." I scanned the ground and found one I'd dropped. Scooping it up, I placed it in my pocket.

"We should go," José said.

I looked at the window. Getting out was going to be harder than getting in. By the time I was sitting in my car, I was ready to call it a day. Sheer determination had gotten me out the window, but I would be bruised and scratched.

José shut his door and turned to me. "You should win a prize. That was some crazy climbing."

"I'm thinking of retiring from climbing through windows." I backed out the car and waved as we passed Boyd and Conan on the bike.

"Probably a good idea."

"I can't figure out what Bill is up to. Why keep money in a shed?"

"What else did you find?"

"Seeds."

"Huh. I didn't think he had a garden."

"They were hidden in one of the wooden statues."

"That's odd."

"I have one in my pocket."

"Boyd might know what it is."

I shook my head. "I understand people hiding money for shady reasons, but seeds?"

"They might grow something illegal."

"If Bill is doing multiple illegal things, why would he tell us about the tax evasion?"

José tapped his hand against the armrest. "Maybe Deputy Russell knew about the tax stuff but not the rest. Bill might have felt like he had to confess to that, just in case Russell had written it down."

"I guess. Bill seems like a nice guy."

"He is, but he's been in trouble with the law a lot since I've known him. He's always trying to make easy money, but not always in the most legal ways."

"His carvings are really good."

"Yeah, but I don't think it brings in a ton of money. He makes a lot at fairs, but those don't come up often."

We pulled into the diner, and José went in. I saw Jett walking down the sidewalk, so I waited for him. I fished the seed from my pocket.

"Hey," he said, scanning me. "What happened to you?"

I looked down. Wood dust covered my bright green shirt. I handed Jett the seed and brushed at the dust. "How did I not notice that?"

"Your arm's all scraped up."

I looked at the side of my arm and shrugged. "It's not bad." I was sure my leg looked worse. I'd scraped it hard on my way down, but I wasn't going to say that.

"What's this?" he asked, holding up the seed.

"It was inside a wooden statue in Bill's shed." I pulled out my phone and showed him a picture of the money. "This was there too, but I left it where it was."

Jett sighed. "Whether Bill is behind Deputy Russell's murder or not, it looks like he's into something."

We looked up when a white car came speeding down the road. Jett frowned and waved his arms, trying to tell them to slow down. The car kept going at its current speed and swerved onto the sidewalk, shooting toward us. Jett grabbed me and pulled back, knocking us both into the diner doorway, causing the car to miss us.

Jett jumped up and held out his hand. I took it and let him pull me up.

"Are you alright?" he asked.

"Yes, you?"

He nodded. "It was a rental car."

My lips pressed into a thin line. "Someone's trying to hurt you. You need to stay in safe places."

A deep crease formed between Jett's eyebrows as worry clouded his face. "Who says I was their target? You need to be careful."

"They're obviously after you," I argued. "I knew it. Russell's death was aimed at you."

"We don't know that. Let's go into the diner. I need to make some calls. If that car goes into Wichita, the police might be able to pick them up."

I nodded and went in. I was beginning to feel sore on my hip, probably from that last fall. My clothes were a disaster. I took Jett upstairs so he could make a call in my quiet kitchen, and I could change into something that hadn't been through a crazy day.

Chapter 14

Once my clothes were changed, I went into the living room and sank into my recliner. I could hear Jett talking from the kitchen, but I couldn't make out what he was saying. My eyes wanted to close, but I kept them open. At least, I thought I did, but then I felt myself opening them when Jett gently shook my shoulder.

"Hey," he said, sitting on the recliner arm. "I don't want you to stay here alone. I'm going to have Boyd stay in your guest room."

I frowned. "No. Then you'll be alone."

"I can take care of myself better than you can."

I raised my brow. "Oh yeah? Like the time you—"

He put his hand over my mouth and smiled. "I don't need a list. I'm not saying you're helpless, but I'm trained, and I have a gun."

"It's more likely someone's after you."

"You never know. You're the one snooping around."

"So are you."

"Yeah, but I'm transparent. People know what I'm doing. You don't follow the rules, so you find out a lot."

"But it's likely they're after you if you go with the theory that they killed Deputy Russell when they were after you."

"Yes, and that's only a theory."

"It's a good one. It makes sense."

"Not if the killer is Bill. He doesn't have anything against me."

"But we don't know it was him. Hanson looks guiltier in my opinion."

"Fine. Boyd can sleep in the guest room, and I'll stay on the sofa. That way, I'll be first to know if someone messes with the door."

I nodded. "That means Conan will have to stay here." Creepers meowed from the other room. I stood and waited for him to come into the room. "Did you hear me bring up Conan?" I squatted down and rubbed his head.

"I'm shocked Creepers seems to like Conan."

I picked my cat up and cuddled him to me. "They have a love-hate relationship. Creepers likes him until he messes with his things."

"I'll call Boyd and tell him to come over."

I placed Creepers on the ground and frowned at my wrist. "My bracelet is gone." I got on my hands and knees and ran my hand over the carpet. Jett stuck his hand around the cushion on the recliner.

"Are you sure you were wearing it?"

"Yes. I remember touching it at Bill's house." I frowned. "I bet it fell off when I went in the window."

"You said you didn't go in the house."

"It was the shed window."

Jett gave me a look that could freeze fire. "I wish you wouldn't go into places like that."

"I need to run back and check."

Jett looked at his watch. "Bill might be home. There's a good chance he won't know it's yours, even if he finds it."

I bit my lip. I'd been wearing that bracelet since Jett gave it to me. Everyone I'd been around probably saw it. Even if they hadn't, I wanted it back.

"I'll go tomorrow. I bet he's too busy with the fair to go work in his shed."

Jett sighed. "We can talk later. I'm going to go to the B&B to see if Hanson and Brooke were there when we almost got ran over."

I nodded, still nervous about the bracelet.

He got up and took my arms in his hands, and his eyes searched mine. "After I do that, I'll go ask Bill to let me walk around his property, maybe show me in the shed. I'll look for the bracelet. I know if I don't, you'll be there in the middle of the night."

A frown etched my face. He wasn't wrong. "I don't want you over there alone. What if Bill was the one who tried to run us over?"

"I doubt he was back from the fair."

"But he could have been."

"I'll take Ledford."

"Okay."

He kissed me and rushed out.

I thought about going to check on the diner, but José always had everything under control. I got into my pajamas and sprawled across my bed. I rubbed my temples and tried to focus. It seemed like too many things pointed at both Hanson and Bill. When I thought about Hanson, I was sure he was guilty—until I thought about Bill. Then it seemed to obviously be him.

Creepers hopped up on the bed and curled up at my side. "I should take advice from you. Just forget about it all and sleep." Creepers ignored me and closed his eyes. "Oh no. Boyd and Jett will be back, so I can't sleep."

Creepers batted at me. I was probably moving too much for his comfort.

"I can't stay awake. They both have a key, so I won't worry about it." I got up, annoying Creepers, and put a pillow and blanket on the couch for Jett. That way, he wouldn't have to wake me up for anything. I got back in bed and pulled my comforter up to my chin and ignored all my pains from the day. Creepers jumped off the bed and went to the window seat. He must figure I wasn't going to stop bothering him.

"Ivs?" Jett's voice broke through my thoughts.

I groaned. "I put a blanket on the couch."

"It's morning."

"What are you talking about?" I asked, not opening my eyes. "I just got in bed."

"Boyd and I came last night, and you were out cold."

I pried my eyes open and scowled at the sun shining through the curtains. "I would have sworn I didn't even fall asleep yet."

"I'm going to the fair in about twenty minutes. Do you want a ride?"

"Yes," I said, sitting up. My entire body was sore from yesterday. I might never go through a shed window again. "Let me get ready."

He nodded and left the room. I got ready as quickly as I could, took some pain meds, and before I knew it, I was in Jett's truck headed for the fair.

"Did you talk to Hanson?" I asked, adjusting my blond ponytail.

"Yeah. He was at the B&B playing foosball. Miss Medley and the man he was playing with vouched for him."

"So it wasn't him."

"The car is his."

I scrunched my forehead. "What?"

"The car that almost hit us is a rental, and it's Hanson's."

"But he wasn't driving it?"

"Not according to him or Miss Medley. Brooke was sitting in the corner, watching him."

"So someone stole his rental and tried to hit us?"

"That's what it sounds like."

"Did you check inside?"

"Yep. I had some people come out last night. There were lots of fingerprints. It was worse than the prints on your cake display. The rental place must not sanitize between customers."

"Were any Bill's?"

"No."

I sighed. "This is so frustrating."

Jett grinned and looked over his sunglasses. "I thought you thrived on this kind of thing."

"Not when it means you're in danger."

"Don't worry. I'm being careful."

"Did you go to Bill's?"

"Not last night. I went this morning, but he was already gone. I looked all around the shed and shined a light in the window. I couldn't see the bracelet."

"I haven't checked my car. It could have fallen off in there. That's the last place I remember it. I bet the fair never lets me come again since I only sold things on two of the days."

"I'm sure they would. You paid, so they aren't losing anything."

"Have you searched the garbage behind the B&B?"

"No. Why?"

"I don't know. Clues?"

"I don't think it could be Hanson. He wasn't at the fair when someone threw the rock, and he wasn't in the car that tried to hit us."

We drove the rest of the way in silence as we were both lost in thought. When we got to the fair, Jett went off to patrol around before the gates opened, and I went over to the spot where my canopy had been. Nothing was there now, not even police tape. They must have taken anything important.

Perry was walking around, swinging a thin tree branch with one arm. I'd forgotten to tell Jett that José thought someone should investigate him.

I waved. "Hi, Perry."

His face lit up. "Ivy. I didn't think you would be back."

"How are things going around here?"

"Quiet compared to the first of the week. Did they ever find out who killed Deputy Russell?"

"Not yet."

"It's too bad I didn't see anything."

"It is. Everyone was distracted at the same time."

"I'm glad they've stopped questioning everyone. That Sheriff Malone almost had me confessing to something I didn't do. That guy scares me."

I laughed. "Jett scares you? He's harmless."

"It doesn't feel that way when he towers over me with his eyes on fire, not looking away. He's much more intimidating than Deputy Russell, but not mean."

My smile faded. "He's nothing like Russell was. He's just trying to get to the bottom of the murder."

He grinned. "I guess you're as gone on the sheriff as every other female around here."

"What do you mean?"

"I can't tell you how many women I've seen following him around trying to get his attention. He ignores all of them, but they keep trying."

"He better ignore all of them," I huffed. I try not to be jealous, but it creeps up sometimes.

Jett came around the corner and smiled, but it quickly turned into confusion. He walked over and gave me a questioning look. "What's wrong?"

I crossed my arms. "Perry was just telling me about the herd of women who keep following you around here."

Jett laughed. "That's ridiculous."

"Hi, Sheriff," a woman said, walking past.

Jett nodded at her, and I raised my eyebrow.

"All she did was say hi."

"You're so cute and clueless."

Jett grinned. "I have to go over by the animals. Do you want to escort me so no one dares to say hi to me?"

My lips twitched. "I trust you."

"Good. See you in a few." He nodded at Perry and walked off.

"I see how things are," Perry said, smiling. "I still say he's intimidating."

"That's his job."

"He does it well."

Chapter 15

This day would go down in history as the longest Fourth of July ever. Being at a fair alone was boring. I should have brought my own car so I could leave, but I would have to stay until after the fireworks. I talked to Jett a few times, and we had lunch together, but I was bored.

I watched a kid who couldn't be older than five get off the Ferris wheel and beg to go again. I hadn't tried going on a Ferris wheel since high school, so maybe it wasn't as bad as I remembered. Taking a deep breath, I walked up and handed someone my ticket. I climbed into a seat and tried to calm my heart. Today, I would conquer the Ferris wheel.

Being scared of Ferris wheels didn't make sense. I wasn't scared of heights, just the way it thrust a person forward. I wanted to get off, but if five-year-olds could enjoy this, so could I. I clenched the bar in front of me so hard my knuckles turned white.

"Can I join you?" someone said. I looked up to see Bill. I didn't want anyone next to me, but I didn't want to be rude. He didn't wait for my answer before just sitting beside me.

"What about your booth?"

"I have a friend watching it."

Our seat jerked backward, and I took a shaky breath. This was a stupid idea. The seat rocked as we went higher.

"Breathe," Bill said. "You aren't scared, are you?"

I didn't look at him. My focus didn't leave my hands. "A little."

"It's completely safe."

"I know." The worst part was ahead. We went over the top, and as we began going down, I closed my eyes. I couldn't force myself to open them. On the second time around, my stomach started roiling.

The ride stopped, and I could feel the seat swinging back and forth.

"Don't close your eyes, or you'll get sick," Bill said.

It was too late. I was terrified, and I was going to puke.

"Why does it have to stop?" I muttered.

"To let more people on. Focus on something in the distance. It can help with the nausea."

I looked out at the pink sky. The sun would be gone soon.

"I've had some trouble lately," Bill said. "Money trouble, mostly."

"Huh," I said, swallowing. Did Bill really have to do this right now? If something didn't change, my lunch hot dog would be on everything.

"I've done a few things I'm not proud of."

"The tax evasion?" I managed to get out.

"Among other things." He moved back and forth, making our seat rock more.

"Stop it!" I commanded, sending him a death glare.

"Right, sorry."

I covered my face with my hands. They were trembling, and everything in me wanted to heave. Motion sickness on top of being terrified was a horrid feeling.

"What have you done that's so bad?" I asked, trying to focus on anything but this churning inside me.

"Nothing awful. It would be nice if people could turn a blind eye to it. It's not hurting anyone, and it will all be gone soon."

"Hmm."

The ride started again.

"It would be easy to fall. That's why I hate these things," he said.

I glared up at him. He didn't look concerned at all. He smiled at me.

When we got near the ground, I turned to the person controlling the ride and yelled, "Hey, I need to get off."

The boy who was probably sixteen just shrugged, and we began going around again.

"I'm going to puke on his shoes," I mumbled.

Bill laughed, and I wanted to punch him. I would puke on him as well if he didn't stop. The boy didn't stop us the next time either. If I didn't know any better, I would think he was doing it on purpose.

I pulled out my phone and dialed Jett. I put the phone up to my ear and fought back my tears. I felt terrible.

"Hey, Ivs."

"I'm on the Ferris wheel. They won't stop, and I'm gonna puke."

"I'm coming."

Sweat rolled down my back, and I grabbed my shirt and moved it back and forth to get some cooler air. I realized Bill was still talking but didn't know what he'd been saying.

"Don't take that as a threat," he said.

I looked up at him with a sharp glare. "What?"

He held out his hand and dropped my bracelet onto my lap. I grabbed it and looked at the crowd. Jett was talking to the boy in control of the ride. When we got to the bottom, it stopped.

Bill stood and looked at me. "Remember what I said."

I stood, and Jett ran over and helped me off the ride. I jumped down and took a deep breath. The boy at the controls looked like he'd been properly reprimanded and had the decency to look at his feet when we passed.

"Are you alright?" Jett asked.

"I will be." I pulled my bracelet over my hand. "Bill had my bracelet. I think he threatened me, but I wasn't listening."

"I saw him take off. You don't know what he said?"

"He said something about doing things he wasn't proud of and something about getting money. That's all I got. I was trying not to puke."

"Come on. I'll get you something to drink." He put his arm over my shoulders, and we walked. He bought me a soda. The area was clearing out since everyone was making their way over to watch the fireworks.

"Feel any better?" Jett asked.

"A lot. I'm never getting on one of those things again. I've said that before, but I'm serious this time."

"I want to keep making rounds during the fireworks. You can go watch without me."

"I'd rather walk with you." I sipped my soda and wished I was in Muddy Creek going through the garbage at the B&B. I smiled at the thought. My life was so different from a little over a year ago.

"Do you think Bill was confessing?"

"No. I think he was saying he was doing something suspicious in his shed and wanted me to keep it to myself."

Jett nodded. "That makes sense. Especially if he isn't the killer."

"Did you check for his prints on the steering wheel of Hanson's car?"

"His weren't there."

The first fireworks burst across the sky. We stopped and stared up at the blue-and-gold blast. We watched for a few minutes, then moved on. I'd always liked fireworks, but I never watched an entire show. I was always too tired.

"Can I have your keys?" I asked. "I think I left my lip balm inside your truck."

He handed me the keys, and I went out to the crowded parking lot. It wasn't hard to find Jett's truck in a crowd. I just had to look for the ugly gray Cybertruck. I knew they were supposed to be the new cool thing, but I thought it looked like a toy that someone made life-sized.

I weaved through the cars and saw Perry standing by the truck. He turned, and his eyes went wide when he spotted me. He was holding something in his hand that he quickly dropped to the side.

"Hello," I said. "I just need to get something from the truck."

He pointed at a flat tire. "I was doing my rounds in the lot and noticed someone slashed this tire. Is this your vehicle?"

I squatted down next to the tire and frowned. Now it would take us even longer to get home. "It belongs to the sheriff."

"Oh. We better go get him." He held up a utility knife. "I found this when I was walking around. It was a few rows down, but it might be the tool they used to do it."

I nodded and pulled a bag from my purse and held it open. "Put it in here so it doesn't get any more prints."

He dropped it inside and fidgeted with his hands. I put the knife in the truck and locked it.

"Do you ever go to Muddy Creek?" I asked as we walked toward the fair.

"Occasionally. I'm from a smaller town, so I shop there."

That seemed weird to me. I did most of my shopping in Wichita because the store in Muddy Creek was so small. Still, a small store was better than no store, and several towns in the county were too small for any businesses.

"Have you been to my diner?"

He raised his eyebrows. "Do you own Sue's Diner?"

"Yes."

"I've been a few times. It was nice."

"Have you been to Muddy Creek lately? I feel like I saw you there," I lied.

He scratched his head. "I can't remember."

Perry didn't strike me as the type to slash someone's tires, but he looked guilty, and he'd been holding a knife.

His story might be true, but it seemed odd that he would happen upon the utility knife and the truck tire. The tire didn't stand out unless you were behind the truck or to the side, and a car blocked it from most people's view.

When we got to the fairgrounds, Perry looked around. "I better go patrol. I'll see you later."

I nodded and searched for Jett. He was walking slowly through the livestock. He wasn't hard to find since there weren't a lot of people over here.

"Did you find it?" he asked.

"What?"

"Your lip stuff."

"Oh no, I forgot about that. Someone slashed one of your tires. There was a utility knife nearby. I don't know if that's what they used, but Perry found it, so I locked it in the truck."

Jett's shoulders slumped. "Man. We aren't catching a lot of breaks. I'm ready to go to sleep, not change a tire. I was up too late last night."

"At least the fair is over after tonight."

He nodded. "Next year, I'm sending one of my deputies and staying as far from it as I can."

"Do we need to call a tow truck?" I asked.

"No, I have a spare in the back."

"I can change it while you patrol," I offered.

He grinned. "Do you know how?"

"I think I did it once in driver's ed. I can google it."

He chuckled. "I'll do it before we leave."

I frowned.

"Don't get insulted," he said. "I just don't want the tire to fall off when we're driving."

"Fine." I didn't want to do it anyway. I just thought it might be faster than waiting. "How much longer until we can go?"

"About thirty minutes."

"It's pretty dead over here."

"Yeah. Everyone likes fireworks."

"They're okay," I said, putting my hands on his shoulders. I leaned in and gave him a soft kiss.

Half his mouth turned up. "Are you saying you want to make our own fireworks?" He didn't wait for my response. He leaned in and kissed me. Explosions sounded all around, but I didn't notice.

Chapter 16

The sun was just beginning to come out, and no one was stirring. I walked down the peaceful street and over to the B&B. The garbage was kept out back in an enormous metal bin. I went over and pulled the heavy top open. It creaked and seemed to echo across town. That was probably my imagination.

I wrinkled my nose as the smell of garbage hit me. I must have disturbed about a million flies because they began flying around my head. The bin was high. I thought about changing my mind and going back, but the garbage would be collected in a couple of days, and it would only get worse.

I looked around and spotted a crate to the side of the bin. I grabbed it and moved it around so I could step on it.

I stepped up and waved my hands around to scare off the flies. They didn't seem to care.

"Gonna jump in?"

I turned around and almost fell off the crate. José stood there smiling. He wore a gray tank top and shorts. I forgot he went running so early. I'd gone with him a few times and given up on it.

"You know I am," I said.

"Why?" He came closer and looked in.

"Just to see if there's anything suspicious."

"I thought Jett was watching you so you didn't do anything like this."

"Jett is sound asleep on my couch. He's had a long week."

José opened the second top to the large dumpster, and more flies assaulted us. I pulled myself over the top and dropped into the bin.

"Let me know if you find anything valuable," José teased.

I scrunched my nose as the bag I was standing on mushed around my feet. "I will, but I'm keeping it."

"Don't hurt yourself."

"I'm collecting bruises this week. My legs are covered. I was so clumsy getting in and out of Bill's shed."

"If we're here, does that mean you're leaning toward Hanson and not Bill?"

"No. Bill is guilty of a lot of things, but I don't think he's the killer. I could be wrong. He was creeping me out yesterday." I kicked some things around and slipped onto my knees. Whatever I was on was cold and seeping through my jeans. I tossed some bags that didn't look too dirty.

"Do you want me to come in?" José asked.

"No. Then it will be crowded and gross. I only want to deal with one."

I moved around one garbage bag after another, not seeing anything interesting. It might be hard to know without dumping them all.

I picked up a small garbage bag and held it up to see inside. It looked like a pair of shoes and something else. I picked the bag open and pulled out the shoes and smiled. I stood and held them up so José could see.

"White Adidas with blue stripes."

José raised one brow. "You think they belong to the person in the black hoodie?"

I pulled a black hoodie from the same bag. "Yep." I handed the stuff to José, then ungracefully pulled myself out of the bin and onto the hard-packed dirt. "I'm going to go show Jett."

"It's early. You aren't going to let him sleep?"

"I might."

"I'm going to finish my run so I can get to the diner on time."

We went our separate ways. This had to be the clues I needed. I went up the steps to my apartment and did my best to turn the key quietly. I walked in and was startled to see Jett hopping in the middle of the room while pulling on his shoe and dodging a hyper Conan.

"Where were you?" he asked, dropping his foot.

I held up the shoes and hoodie. "The garbage."

Jett studied the shoes. "At the B&B?"

"Yep."

I handed them to him, and he turned them around. He looked at the tongue. "Size 8. I doubt Hanson wears a size 8. I bet this is a woman's shoe."

I frowned. The person in the hoodie could have been a woman. I'd never gotten close enough to know. I looked at the hoodie. "This is a men's large."

"It might be a coincidence you found these. Anyone could throw away shoes and a hoodie."

"But in the same bag? And look at those shoes. They aren't old."

He nodded and placed them on the couch. "You know I love you, right?"

I tilted my head. "Yeah?"

"You smell terrible."

I tried to glare, but it turned into a smile. "I ruined these pants. I don't even want to know what's on the knees. You should have seen the flies. I was worried they might carry me away."

He smiled. "Go take a shower."

"What are you going to do?"

"I'll call someone to see if they can get prints off the shoes. They aren't smooth, so it might be difficult."

After my second shower of the day, I went looking for Brooke. If the shoes belonged to the person at the fair and were a woman's size, my bet was on her. I found Hanson sitting in the game room at the B&B, playing pool with two other people I didn't know.

"Hi, Ivy," he said, looking up from his shot. "Do I want to know why you're here?"

"I need to talk to Brooke."

"She's at the library. Why do you need her?"

I shrugged. I wasn't going to hash it out with Hanson first.

"I hope you aren't expecting anything from her. She's being stubborn lately."

"Oh yeah?"

"She keeps disappearing and won't tell me where. It's not like her."

"Does she own a pair of Adidas?"

He took a shot and frowned. "Why would I know what her shoes look like?"

"Because you're with her all the time."

"I'm not a shoe person. I don't stare at people's feet."

"Well, do you know if she has a black hoodie?"

"I know she took mine and won't give it back."

I rubbed my lips together. That was all I needed. "Thanks." I turned and rushed from the room.

When I got to the sidewalk, Hanson came running out. "Ivy, wait!"

I stopped and looked impatiently at him.

"Why do you care about all this stuff?"

"It has nothing to do with you. Don't worry about it."

"I can't imagine why you need to know what brand Brooke's shoes are."

"I like shoes," I said. It was true, but it had nothing to do with anything.

He looked confused but went back inside. I hurried over to the library. The glass doors opened, and I went inside.

"Hey, Ivy," Brian, the librarian, said.

"Hello. How are things?"

"Pretty good. It's the busy month." He grinned and raked his hand through his black curls. "By busy, I mean at least three people come in every day."

I laughed. "I see more than three people now."

"Yeah, it's a good time. Are you looking for something specific?"

I walked close to his desk and leaned close. "Is there a woman in here with long black hair?"

"There was, but she left about five minutes ago." His smile faded. "Please tell me she isn't a suspect in a murder or anything? I got her number."

I tilted my head. "On purpose?"

"Of course on purpose."

"Did you talk to her first?"

"Yes. For almost a half hour."

"Hmm. I guess everyone has their own taste."

"She's a suspect, isn't she?"

I nodded, and he let out a long breath. "Do you know how long it's been since I've been on a date? I should have gotten married when I was younger. Now I'm left with murder suspects."

"You aren't too old. Your problem is you live in a small town with few options."

"I guess. So you think she killed the deputy?"

"I'm not sure."

"I have the worst taste."

"She might be innocent. Even if she's not, she's not very nice."

"Really? She seemed friendly."

"I guess I only know how she interacts with me."

"She said she's from Arizona." His eyes went wide. "Right. You're from Arizona."

I leaned against the desk. "She's best friends with a guy I dated. I'm not her favorite person."

"Does she like him?"

"Yeah."

"Then why did she give me her number?"

I shrugged. "Maybe she's given up on him."

His eyes flickered to the door. "She's coming back." I didn't turn. I was sure I would look like I'd just been gossiping about her.

She stood next to me and smiled at Brian. "Hey, Brian? I was thinking, maybe we could catch dinner sometime before I leave?"

Brian smiled, but it looked forced. "Sure. That would be great."

"Can I talk to you for a minute?" I asked.

Brooke rolled her eyes. "I'm done talking to you."

Brian looked uncomfortable.

"I have a new toy for Creepers," Brian said, pulling a sack out from under the desk.

"You spoil him," I said, taking it.

"I know, but I feel like his godfather or something like that."

"Well, thanks. He loves everything you get him."

I wanted to take Brooke somewhere to talk, but it didn't look like she was going to go for it.

"You owe me a new cake stand," I told her.

She twitched slightly, and her face went blank. "Why?"

"Because you broke my last one, and it was brand new."

Brooke chewed the inside of her lip. "I never touched it."

"No, but your rock did."

"I have no idea what you're talking about."

"You know the police think whoever threw that rock probably killed Deputy Russell?"

"Well, I didn't throw it, so I'm not worried."

"You threw your shoes and Hanson's hoodie you wore in the garbage. They're being fingerprinted right now."

She folded her arms and rubbed them. "Throwing my clothes away doesn't make me a criminal."

"No, but committing a crime while you were wearing them does. Several people saw you."

Brooke turned and bolted across the library. I took off after her, with Brian at my heels. She ran out the door and down the street. She wasn't going to get away in her strappy sandals. I grabbed her arm and swung her around, almost losing my balance.

"Knock it off!" she yelled.

"You can walk to the sheriff's office, or we can call him," Brian said.

Her eyes narrowed. "Delete my number from your phone."

"I'm planning on it."

"I'll call Jett," I said.

"You can't stop me from leaving," she said. "You have no authority."

She was right, but it hadn't ever stopped me before.

"I'm going back to my room." She stomped in the direction of the B&B.

We followed her, and I called Jett. He said he would meet us. When we got to the B&B, Jett was already pulling up in his truck. He got out, his eyes focused on Brooke.

"What's happening?" he asked.

"Ivy's trying to blame things on me!" Brooke accused.

"What things?" he asked.

"She was the one in the hoodie. It was Hanson's hoodie, but she took it and didn't give it back," I explained.

"That doesn't mean I did anything."

I looked at Jett. "My guess is she's the one who tried to run us over the other day."

"What are you talking about? I was sitting, reading when that happened. Even the sheriff knows that. He came over after it happened."

"I didn't ask Miss Medley if Brooke had been there when I asked about Hanson," Jett said. "I'll have to ask her and Hanson."

"Do you need me here?" Brian asked.

"I think we're covered," Jett said.

Brooke glared at Brian. "I can't believe I thought you were a nice guy."

"He is a nice guy," I said.

Her brows came together. "You sure seemed to think so. That's probably why you're accusing me. You never think I should get to talk to any guys worthwhile."

"That's ridiculous," I said. "You're the one who won't tell Hanson you like him."

Brian waved and went back toward the library.

Jett put a hand to his chin. "I suppose we can check the fingerprints on the rock that broke your cake stand. See if they match Brooke's."

I tilted my head and looked at Jett. We didn't know where the rock was. Tons of rocks covered the fairgrounds. Jett's eyes were focused on Brooke. He was bluffing.

She shifted. "Fine. I threw the rock. Happy, Ivy?"

"And you tried to run us over?" Jett prodded.

She leveled him with a sharp glare.

"I'll ask at the B&B. If everyone can vouch for you, I'll believe it."

She shifted from one foot to the other. "Okay, so I did that too. I wasn't really going to hit you. That's all I did, though. My admitting that proves I didn't do the rest."

Jett pulled out his handcuffs and shook his head. "It doesn't prove anything."

"You can't handcuff me and drag me through town! I didn't do anything to get arrested for."

"Why did you do any of it?"

She pulled on her hair and scowled. "I wanted you to know Hanson wasn't there when those things happened. I knew people could prove he'd been somewhere else."

"Why would you want to do that?"

She looked up at the sky and took a deep breath. "Because then you wouldn't realize he killed the deputy."

Chapter 17

I paced across the diner kitchen. As soon as Brooke made her declaration, she refused to say anything else. Jett took her to the small jail attached to his office for attempting to run us over. I'd barely slept all night, and now I was restless.

I grabbed some butter and put it in a mixing bowl, then I paced for a few more minutes. Brooke had pretty much said that she thought Hanson had done it. Or maybe she knew. Since she wouldn't talk and clarify anything, it was all a guess.

"What are you doing with that butter?" José asked.

"Making cookies."

"We don't need any."

I nodded and covered the butter with plastic wrap and put it back in the fridge. I went back to my pacing.

José stepped in front of me. "Do you need help with anything?"

"I can't put this case together. Some things feel like they should be glaringly obvious."

Carrie pulled some chicken from the fryer. "I bet you need a rest. No one can think right on the amount of sleep you get."

"I think I sleep enough."

José took a pastry brush and used it to rub melted butter over a pan of rolls. "You were up before six dumpster diving."

"You were up."

"That's the only time I can run."

"Both of you need to relax more," Carrie said. Her eyes rested on José, then jumped away. I frowned and wondered when José would notice Carrie's interest in him. I'd told him once, but he didn't believe me. Just like when I tried to tell Hanson about Brooke.

"José does," I said. "From now on, José isn't allowed to work longer than nine hours a day."

"What?" he exclaimed. "What am I supposed to do for the rest of the day?"

"Have fun."

"Doing what?"

I shrugged. "Whatever you want."

He opened his mouth to protest but stopped when I gave him an icy stare. "If you don't like that, I'll make you work forty hours a week like a normal person."

"Fine."

"Tiffany wants more hours," Carrie said.

"Great," I said. "I'll talk to her next time she's in."

Jett came into the kitchen, and his eyes stopped on me. "I have a bunch of people in my office. Can you come? I might need your views on what happened."

I nodded and took off my hairnet and apron.

"I might need José as well."

"Don't you usually talk to one person at a time?" Carrie asked.

"Yes, and I did, but I wonder if I might get further if they're all together."

José and I followed him out.

"I finally found out what that seed was you found in Bill's shed," Jett said over his shoulder.

"What?"

"It's from a coca plant."

"Like Fran was growing?"

"Yep."

"Do that many people make illegal tea?" I asked.

"Coca plants are also the source of cocaine," José told me.

"Right. Fran said something about that. So Bill was evading taxes and supplying people with drugs?"

Jett nodded. "It looks that way. He's not admitting to the drug part yet. I sent Ledford to his house, and the entire shed is gone."

"I should have taken more pictures."

"The picture of the money will be helpful. It proves he was hiding something. I still have the seed as well."

"I guess he didn't admit to killing Deputy Russell?"

"No."

We walked up to the sheriff's office and went in. Hanson, Bill, and Perry were all waiting in chairs.

"Come on." Jett motioned to them. "Follow me into the back." They all stood, and we walked past Jane at her desk and went through a doorway and into the area with cells. Brooke was sitting in one on a small bed. She looked ready to punch someone.

Jett opened the empty cell and motioned to Bill.

Bill's lips tightened, but he went in.

"This is only temporary," Jett said. "I need to have some control." He shut the cell and called out the door. "Ledford? Can you join us?"

Deputy Ledford came in and shut the door. This place needed more cells.

A small pathway with two chairs went in front of the cells. Jett had Hanson and Perry sit in them. Ledford went over to stand by Hanson.

"We're all going to stay calm, alright?" Jett said.

No one responded.

"I've brought you all here because you are all suspects in the murder of Deputy Russell."

"I'm a suspect?" Perry asked.

"Sorry, Perry," Jett said. "You did tell people of your dislike of Russell, and you were by my slashed tires. We have to be thorough."

"I understand."

Jett peered into Brooke's cell. "Brooke, you admitted to throwing the rock at Ivy's table and trying to run us down with Hanson's rental car."

"What?" Hanson asked, his eyes focused on Brooke.

Brooke didn't say anything.

"You also said you did it so we wouldn't think Hanson was behind the killing. Why would you think he needed an alibi?"

"Seriously, Brooke," Hanson said. "You tried to run them over? Why? Does that mean you killed the deputy as well?"

Fire flashed in Brooke's eyes. "I did it so you wouldn't look guilty! What is anyone supposed to think? Someone's murdered, and you are covered in the cheesecake that was all over the murder scene! When I asked you about it, you wouldn't talk."

"You think I did it?"

Brooke shrugged.

"Did you?" Jett asked.

Hanson crossed his arms. "Of course not."

"I didn't do it either," Perry said. "I was just in the wrong place."

Jett turned to Bill. "Bill's and Hanson's stories don't line up. Bill says he felt someone crawl under his table. Hanson says no one was at Bill's table when he went under it."

Hanson's leg bounced nervously up and down. "If I tell you what happened, will you promise to keep Bill away from me?"

Bill held the bars and narrowed his eyes. "You have nothing on me."

"He won't be allowed near you," Jett said.

Hanson looked at Jett. "I'm not kidding. I want protection."

"Alright."

"I went over to Ivy's table. No one was there. I went behind it because I'd been eyeing the cheesecake. I took a piece and ate it while I stood there. I figured it was the end of the day, so Ivy wouldn't need it. I grabbed an empty pie tin and put the rest of the cake inside. Deputy Russell came over and saw me. He told me he could have me arrested for stealing. I was nervous, and I dropped the cheesecake."

"And?" I asked. I wasn't as patient as Jett.

"The deputy told me to clean it up. I got down on the ground and started picking it up. That's when I saw Bill step up from the side and hit Deputy Russell over the head."

"That's a lie!" Bill exclaimed. "It's his word against mine."

"Quiet," Jett commanded. "You'll have your turn."

Hanson wiped sweat from his head. "I panicked. I wasn't sure whether Bill saw me or not. I scrambled under the table, crawling over the cheesecake. That's why it was all over me. I waited quietly until he left, then crawled under the tables. I got out and ran to the car and left."

"Why didn't you come forward earlier?"

"I had no proof, and I knew I looked guilty. I had cheesecake everywhere, and all I had was my word."

"Bill?" Jett asked. "What happened that night?"

"Nothing. The fireworks started, and I went home. I didn't see or do anything. That guy's a liar."

"I'm not."

Jett sighed. "I'm keeping you here for a while, Bill."

"I didn't do it."

"I have enough other stuff on you to keep you."

"Who slashed Jett's tire?" I asked.

Bill moved his lips from side to side. He looked as guilty as anything I'd seen but didn't speak.

Jett looked pointedly at Bill. "I have someone running the utility knife for prints."

"Can I go?" Perry asked.

Jett nodded. "Everyone can go except Bill and Brooke."

I walked back to the diner with José, and Hanson followed us. When we got to the diner, José went into the kitchen, and Hanson sank down into a booth. I sat across from him.

"I don't know why Brooke would try to cover for me," he said.

I raised my eyebrow. "It's like I've been telling you. She's in love with you. That's why she always hated me."

He sighed. "I wonder if that's right."

"It is."

"Brooke's always been a good friend, but I doubt we could have a healthy relationship."

"Why? You do everything with her."

"Yeah, but she isn't you."

"And you're going to have to find someone who isn't."

"Yeah, I know. I shouldn't have come. I didn't really think you would take me back. Now I've got Brooke in a mess."

"I doubt she'll get in too much trouble."

"It blows my mind. You think you know someone. I can't be mad, though. She did it for me."

"What will you do now?" I asked.

"I'll wait a few days and see what's going on with Brooke, then I'll go home. I won't bother you again."

"Let me get you some food," I said, getting up.

"Thanks."

I went into the kitchen. Anton and Livy were putting on aprons.

I smiled. "You're back. Was it fun?"

Livy beamed at Anton. "So fun. Anton's family is so nice."

"And they love you," Anton said, pulling on a hairnet.

"How did the fair go?" Livy asked me.

"I made a profit. But I only worked two days."

"Oh?"

"Someone got killed at my booth."

Anton raised his eyebrow. "For reals? Man, you need to come with a warning sign. It should say, 'Hi, I'm Ivy. Don't come near me or you might get murdered.'"

I gave a half smile. "It does seem that way, doesn't it?"

"There is way too much crime in Muddy Creek," Livy said, grabbing a pad of paper. "I wonder if we're on any record books for crimes in a small town."

"It wasn't like that until recently," Anton said.

"I bet it was," José said. "We just didn't know because Ivy wasn't around to pick it all out."

"Well, I've had enough," I said. "Tonight I'm going to bed early, and tomorrow I'm sleeping in, then going to help Barbra declutter her house. That always relaxes me."

Livy grimaced. "I don't see how cleaning relaxes anyone."

"Barbra has so many interesting things. It's fun to go through it. We've almost cleaned her entire first floor. I go by every few days to make sure she hasn't started piling new things up."

José grabbed a rag. "There are probably decades of things in her house."

"Maybe more. The stuff in her attic was there when her family moved in, but she didn't want to clean it out, so it's just been sitting and collecting dust. Who knows what cool things might be stashed away?"

Chapter 18

"You can't tell me you need this." I held up a chipped elephant bookend.

Barbra straightened her purple ponytail and stuck out her lower lip. "I used to love those things. It was a set, but one broke."

"This one's chipped and faded. What are you going to do with it?"

Barbra sighed. "Toss it, I suppose."

"Do you want to take a picture?"

"No. I have a picture from back when it was new."

The small room we were working in wasn't as interesting as the lower floors. Now we were on the second floor, and these were the rooms her kids had been in. Barbra had kept everything they ever made.

I found some big three-ring binders, and we were making one for each child. Barbra could choose the artwork she really wanted to save, and we would keep it in the binders. She'd saved papers with one line drawn in crayon, and all of those went in the trash.

"I can't wait to get to the attic," I said. "Who knows what might be up there?"

"A lot of dust, that's for sure."

"I can't believe you never were curious enough to look."

She shrugged. "I thought about it a few times, but it sounded like a lot of work, and I figure if no one cared enough to take the stuff with them when they moved, it's probably junk."

"Probably, but what if it isn't? Or it might have things that weren't worth anything back then but are now."

"I'm thinking about moving."

I looked up. "Where?"

"To the new condos in town. It would be nice to be closer to people, and if some of them are set aside for a retirement community, I would have people my age. Opal's thinking about it as well."

"How long until they build?"

"I think they're going to start next month. I'm not sure when they plan to be livable. I could sell this place for a lot, buy a condo, and have plenty of money to live on."

"It would be nice to have you closer. You can't move before I see the attic."

"Let's go up now."

"Really?"

Barbra nodded. "Why not? We don't have to clean it, but we could look around. I've been up there a bunch because I stored some things but never moved any of the old stuff around."

I couldn't believe anyone could be so uncurious. I would have been through the entire attic before I was all the way moved in. We went to the hallway, and Barbra opened a door to a dark staircase. She flipped on a light, and we went up. The wooden stairs creaked.

A shiver went up my spine as I wondered what we might find. When we got to the top, a smile spread across my face. It looked just like an attic from the movies. Wooden boxes lined the walls, and the ceiling was peaked at the top and came down on the sides. It was only three feet high in some spots.

I could tell the places Barbra had put her things. Her stuff was in cardboard boxes that looked like they'd been chucked up here without a thought. The wooden boxes were neatly stacked. Neat was not a word that described Barbra.

"I can't believe your kids never searched in here when they were young."

"They came up to play but weren't interested in a bunch of junk. They played hide-and-seek and made a play area."

"I want to bust everything open."

"Just looking at this makes me tired," Barbra said. "I'm going downstairs to make some lemonade."

I nodded and walked over to an old trunk. I'd seen enough movies and read enough books to know that if I was going to find anything, it would be in here. I kneeled in front of it and unlatched it. The dust on top was thick. I pushed the lid open and peered inside.

A folded patchwork quilt took up one side. Next to it was a pile of yellowed envelopes, held together with a faded blue ribbon. I smiled and gently picked them up. This was what I was looking for. I closed the trunk and put the letters on top. I would ask Barbra if I could take them home and read them. Right now, I was going to keep looking.

I pried open a few boxes. One was full of old china. That might be worth something. Another one had crocheted mittens and socks that looked like they'd never been used. Some things I would guess were fifty years old, but some were a lot older.

A tear leaked from my eye, and I rubbed at my nose. The dust was getting to me. I sneezed a few times and decided it was enough for today. I grabbed the pile of yellow envelopes and went down to find Barbra. She was sitting at the kitchen table, sipping lemonade. She scooted another glass toward me.

I sat down and put the letters on the table.

"What are those?" she asked.

"I'm not sure, but I'm excited to find out."

"Go ahead and take them."

I nodded and took a drink. It was sour. "I bet there's a lot of stuff up there you could sell. Some is probably worth a lot."

"You think so?"

I nodded. "I didn't look at most of it, but there is definitely some quality stuff."

"Well, you show me anything interesting when you find it."

"I will."

"What do you think the envelopes have in them?"

I grinned. "I hope they're love letters."

Barbra laughed. "They probably are. What else would a person save, tied up with a ribbon?"

"Do you want to read them first?"

"No. If they're any good, you can show them to me."

"Do you think it's wrong to read someone else's letters?"

"Not if they left them here. Besides, the people are long gone. It's history."

I nodded. "I wish I could read them now, but I have to go help at the diner."

"Can you drive me into town? I'm meeting Opal and the girls at the library."

"You bet."

I took Barbra to the library, then went to the diner. Elvis was playing on the jukebox, but there was only one table of patrons. I put the letters upstairs in my top dresser drawer so Creepers couldn't tear them apart. I wanted to dive in and read them, but they could wait.

I went out the back door and down the stairs. I took a deep breath of the humid Kansas air, then went into the kitchen. I pulled on a purple apron. "What do you need me to do?"

José's sleeves were rolled up, and he was leaning over a boiling pot of pasta. "Can you flip the burgers?"

"Sure." I went over to the skillet, grabbed the spatula, and began turning them.

"We've got a crowd all of a sudden."

I peeked out the serving window. The place was packed. "When I got here, only one table was being used."

"They came together on a bus."

We had tour buses come by occasionally, but they usually called ahead. "A tour bus?"

"No. The company building the condos brought in a bunch of people to see the area. I guess they're trying to sell the small-town life."

Anton handed Livy a plate out the window, then went over to the fryer.

Carrie rushed in the back door and pulled on an apron. "I saw the tour bus."

"Isn't it your day off?" I asked.

"It's okay. I don't want to leave you scrambling."

"What's Muddy Creek going to be like when the condos are full?" I wondered out loud. "If they're building a hundred, and only one person moves into each one, the population here will grow by over ten percent. And you know some will have multiple people."

José pulled the pot off the stove. "It will change things. Perhaps not as much as we think, though, if most of them are retirement neighborhoods."

Time flew by as we scrambled to get everyone fed. When the bus pulled away, we let out a collective sigh.

I sat on a stool. "Thanks for coming, Carrie."

"No problem." She pulled off her apron and hairnet. "I need to get some hobbies, so I have plans on my days off. My only hobby is cooking, so working here is fun for me."

"The condos will be close to the diner. I bet we get a lot more business. We might have to hire more people."

Anton looked over from where he was washing his hands. "I might need to go part-time in a few months. I'm going to start some online college courses. I think I can handle working full-time and classes, but I'm not sure since I've never done it."

I tapped my fingers against the island. "I've been thinking of hiring a few more people anyway so José can get more time off."

"I don't need it," José said.

"Everyone needs time."

"What would I do with it?"

"I don't know. Tinker with cars?"

"Maybe."

Carrie frowned at him. "You could take time to relax every once in a while."

Livy poked her head in the kitchen. "There's a guy who wants to see you, Ivy."

I came out and saw a man with a camera. He raked his hand over his red hair and studied the diner. He appeared to be in his mid-twenties.

"Are you Ivy Clark?" he asked, holding out his hand.

I shook it. "Yes."

"I'm Mac Fanning. I'm taking pictures to include in the brochures for the new condos."

"Nice to meet you."

"Can I take some pictures of your diner?"

"Sure."

"Thanks. Do you have any people who would let me photograph them? Maybe two people sitting at a booth talking?"

"The crowd all left. I can ask one of my cooks and servers to take off their aprons and sit there if you want."

"That would be great."

Livy was standing near me listening.

"Do you mind?" I asked her.

"Nope. Should I get Anton?"

"Yes."

She disappeared into the kitchen.

"This is a nice town you have," Mac said.

"I like it."

"I want to take a picture out front of a couple, preferably kissing. Do you know anyone who might agree to that? I want a big, cozy collage of pictures."

"Hmm." I thought for a minute. There was no way I was going to volunteer to be in any of the pictures. A thought popped into my mind, and I smiled. "I might have someone."

Livy and Anton exited the kitchen as I entered.

"Did you hear about the guy taking pictures?" I asked.

"Yep," José said, placing a pan in the dishwasher.

"He needs some more people. Would you do it?"

José shrugged and kept filling the dishwasher. "Sure."

"You and Carrie?"

Carrie turned and touched her hair. "I guess, but I look like I've been working in the kitchen all day."

"You just have to stand outside the diner. Oh. And kiss."

José dropped a dish, and Carrie's eyes went wide.

"Kiss?" José asked. "That's crazy."

"It's just one little picture," I assured him. "It shouldn't take more than a minute."

José looked at Carrie and chewed on the inside of his cheek. Carrie still hadn't responded.

"Don't you want to make Muddy Creek look good?" I was struggling to hold in a smile. I would never do this if I didn't think it might help my friends.

"Why don't you and Jett do it?" José asked.

"Jett's working."

"Why us?"

"Because he needs someone now, and I don't know any-one else I would dare to ask."

"What about Livy and Anton?"

That made sense, but I wasn't budging. "They're doing a different picture. Come on. Don't be a wimp."

José crossed his arms. "Are you stooping to using peer pressure?"

I grinned. "Maybe."

"Fine, but I don't have all day."

I looked at Carrie. She looked terrified. "Carrie?"

"I suppose I could do it."

"Perfect. Let's go."

We went to the dining area, and I introduced them to Mac. He'd already finished with Anton and Livy, so we went outside. I was sure I didn't need to be there, but I wanted to see what happened.

"Alright, now stand over there," Mac said, motioning toward the large diner window. José and Carrie moved hesitantly to the window. "Great. Now, José, put your hands on her waist. Carrie, rest yours on his shoulders."

I'd never seen two people look so awkward in my life. Carrie put her hands on his shoulders and looked any-where but at José. José took a deep breath and put his on her waist. I wanted to giggle, but I held it in.

Mac put the camera up to his eye. "Okay, now kiss her."

José leaned toward Carrie, and her eyes opened wider than I thought possible.

"Close your eyes, Carrie," I ordered from the side.

She closed her eyes, and José pressed his lips to hers. I wanted to clap, but I controlled myself.

Mac clicked the button a few times. "Keep going until I tell you to stop."

I covered my mouth with one hand, sure my eyes were sparkling. José was either going to love me or kill me at the end of this.

Carrie moved in a little closer, and José's arms moved around to her back.

"Yes, that's better," Mac said, still shooting pictures. "Perfect. You can stop."

They didn't.

"Thanks for your cooperation," Mac told me. "Do you know where I can shoot some good scenery?"

"If you wait until sunset, we get some awesome skies. If you walk down a few blocks, there are some big open areas."

"Great, thanks. Do you serve dessert?"

"Yes, come in and I'll get you something." We moved past José and Carrie and went into the diner.

Livy was staring at José and Carrie from the window. "Do you see this?" she said. "I thought they might like each other but wouldn't ever do anything about it."

I nodded and showed Mac to a booth. "What can I get you?"

"What's the best dessert?"

"They're all good," Livy said, "but Ivy's cookies are the best."

"I'll take one."

I nodded and went to the kitchen.

Anton was the only one there. I grabbed a cookie and took it out.

Mac took a big bite. "Mmm. I could die happily with that in my mouth."

The smile faded from my face.

"Are you alright?" he asked.

"Yes, I just thought of something. Excuse me."

José rushed through the diner and into the kitchen without looking at me. I walked outside and saw Carrie walking down the sidewalk. I looked for cars, then darted across the street and down the next road to the sheriff's office. I'd messed up, and I needed to fix it.

Chapter 19

I opened the door and hurried in.

"Hi, Ivy," Jane said, adjusting her glasses.

I smiled, but it was forced.

"Is Jett here?"

She pointed. "In his office."

I rushed to the door and pulled it open without knocking. Jett looked up from his computer.

"Did Deputy Russell have a cookie in his mouth when he died?"

Jett arched his eyebrow. "Yes. I don't think I can arrest him for stealing at this point."

"Ha-ha. When I first talked to Hanson about the murder, I wondered why Deputy Russell would be at my table.

Hanson said that Russell was eating a cookie when he saw him.”

“Okay?”

“If Hanson’s story about Bill was true, then what about the cookie? Hanson said he dropped down to clean up the cheesecake. If Russell was giving him a hard time for stealing cheesecake, why would he steal a cookie right after? Even if Russell did steal one, Hanson was supposedly bending over, not looking up. He wouldn’t know.”

“So you’re saying Hanson lied.”

“Yes.”

“I’ll go talk to him.”

“I’m coming.”

“You should go to the diner.”

“I can’t. I tricked José and Carrie into kissing, and now I’m scared to talk to José.”

Jett grinned. “How do you trick two adults into kissing?”

“I’ll tell you later. Come on.”

The B&B was quiet, and no one answered when we knocked on Hanson’s door. We went out back and saw Hanson loading things into his rental.

“Hey,” he said, slamming the trunk.

“I didn’t give you permission to leave town,” Jett said.

Hanson shrugged. “I figured since you closed the case, I could go.”

“The case isn’t closed.”

"Oh?"

"I have reason to believe Bill didn't kill Russell."

Hanson swallowed. "But I saw it."

"Did you?"

"Not the details, but yeah."

"Why did you do it, Hanson?" I asked. "Did you think he was Jett?"

He rubbed his lips together. "What are you talking about?"

"You killed Russell. Why?"

Jett took a deep breath, and I expected him to tell me to let him handle it, but he didn't.

"Why would I kill him? I didn't even know him."

"You have a temper occasionally."

He frowned. "I don't get why you think Bill is innocent."

"Because you messed up, Hanson. You made a mistake." I was bluffing. I knew it, and Jett knew it, but I hoped Hanson didn't. He had made a mistake, but it was only my memory of a conversation versus his.

He shifted from one foot to the other. "Ivy—I—It's not—"

I raised my brow. "Yes?"

"What mistake?" he finally said. "I didn't do anything."

"The more you lie, the worse things will be. Come clean and make it easier on yourself."

Hanson sat on his car's bumper and covered his face with his hands. "Deputy Russell came up when I was taking the cheesecake. He was a real jerk. I was already mad about the way he threw me out of the fair. I dropped the cheesecake, and he told me to pick it up. He stuffed a cookie in his mouth like the rules didn't apply to him."

"And?"

"I lost it. I grabbed the cake stand and smashed it over his head. He fell, and I saw someone coming toward the booth. I dropped down and crawled under the tables. I didn't mean to kill him. I didn't even know he died until later."

Jett and I shared a frown.

"You can't blame me. It was an accident."

"But you meant to hit him," Jett said. "You should have come forward immediately. You lied, and you tried to get an innocent person thrown in jail in your place."

Hanson looked up. "He isn't innocent. He's done tons of illegal things."

"Yes, but not murder."

Hanson held out his hands, and Jett cuffed him.

I watched Jett lead him away. I didn't feel up to following. This might be the least satisfactory case I'd solved. Hanson drove me crazy, but I felt bad it had all gone down like this. I wandered back to the diner and into the kitchen.

José was pulling a pan of brownies from the oven. The thought of José and Carrie made me smile. He turned and looked at me.

"What?" he asked.

"Nothing."

He gave me a partial smile. "Don't try to look innocent. I know you enjoyed every second of that."

"I really, really did." I grinned mischievously. "Did you?"

He grumbled something under his breath.

"What was that?"

"You don't want to know."

I folded my arms and did a horrible job of pretending to look cross. "If you remember correctly, you teased me endlessly before I started dating Jett."

"That was different. Everyone knew the two of you were pining after each other."

"What the heck does 'pining' mean?" Anton asked from where he was stirring batter.

I giggled. "It means José is an old guy who isn't hip with the new cool words."

Anton grinned. "I hate to tell you this, Ivy, but 'hip' isn't all that hip these days. You might be getting older yourself."

"I'm what? Five years older than you?"

"What did you do to José?"

"I didn't do anything. I asked him to help a photographer out, and he agreed. He can't blame that on me."

José pointed at me. "Now Carrie's going to avoid me like the plague."

"No, she won't."

"She took off pretty fast."

"That's because she likes you."

"You're crazy."

Anton threw his hands in the air. "Come on, people. Tell me what happened."

"José kissed Carrie," I said, remembering all the times José, Boyd, and Anton teased me.

"It's about time."

"What?" José protested. "It wasn't a real kiss. It was just for a brochure."

I smiled. "Yes, but you were getting into it at the end."

José looked ready to argue, then he sighed. "I guess I was."

"I can take over, and you can go talk to her."

"She's too young for me."

"Once a person's an adult, age doesn't matter anymore." I wasn't sure how old Carrie was, but I guessed her early forties. Since José was fifty, they couldn't be that far apart.

"I don't need the distraction. I bet she quits now."

"Not if you go talk to her."

"About what?"

I rolled my eyes. "About your feelings?"

"I'm not a 'talk about your feelings' kind of guy."

"But you could be."

The door opened, and Carrie walked in. She looked at José and opened her mouth like she was going to speak, then shut it and walked back out.

"Go after her!" I urged.

José sighed and rushed out the door.

I stared at the door and bit my lip.

"It's killing you not to listen, isn't it?" Anton teased.

"Yes. I hope it works out."

I was doing my best to block out my thoughts about Hanson. I'd probably teased José more than I normally would in hopes of distracting myself. I pressed my ear to the door.

"You aren't going to hear anything. When they did the remodel, they made that door solid."

"I know." I sighed. "José isn't going to tell me anything."

I heard someone walking overhead. "It sounds like Boyd is upstairs." I grinned slyly. "I should probably go up and check on him."

Anton crossed his arms and smiled at me. "You know you can go up there without going out back."

I stuck out my tongue. "Fine."

He laughed, and I walked through the diner, up the stairs, and into my apartment. I hurried into the living room. The windows in there looked behind the diner, so I might be able to see something. I pulled the curtains back and scanned the area. José and Carrie were facing each other, talking. I frowned. José had his arms crossed. That wasn't reassuring.

"Who are you spying on?" Boyd asked, coming from the kitchen.

"José and Carrie."

Boyd joined me at the window. "What are they doing?"

"Just talking, it looks like."

"What else would they be doing?"

"A photographer is in town taking pictures for a brochure. I got José and Carrie to stand in front of the diner and kiss. I was hoping it would kick José into gear. I might have just made them awkward."

Boyd laughed. "I wish I'd seen it."

"I hope I didn't put the two of them together in my mind when there wasn't anything there, but I'm almost sure they like each other." I wasn't completely sure about José, but I felt fairly confident about Carrie.

"José's been on his own so long he probably doesn't know what to do. I'm just glad you stopped trying to get me with Barbra."

"You like her," I said, not taking my eyes off José and Carrie.

"I do, but we would be awful together. She'd boss me to death."

José dropped his arms, then held them open. Carrie stepped over, and he gave her a hug.

I moved my lips to the side in frustration. It was better than nothing.

"It's a friend hug," Boyd said. "I bet they just decided to be friends."

"No," I muttered. "It's lasting longer than a friend hug."

"How long does a friend hug last?"

"A few seconds."

José pulled slightly away and said something to her. She stared up at him and nodded. He leaned over and kissed her.

"Yes!" I jumped up in the air and pumped my arm, letting the curtains fall shut.

Boyd chuckled. "If you ever get tired of detective work, you can open a matchmaker's shop."

I flopped back onto the recliner. "I should probably stop. If all my workers fall in love, we'll never get anything done. Anton and Livy sneak out back every chance they get. Now they'll have to compete with those two."

Creepers jumped up on my lap and crawled up on my shoulder. He rested his head on mine.

"Is that really comfortable?" I asked him. He purred and smacked me in the face with his tail. "I left Anton alone in the kitchen."

Boyd looked out the window. "It looks like José went back in." He quickly pushed the curtains closed and looked around guiltily. "Carrie's coming up."

I pulled Creepers off my head and pushed my hair down.

"Let her in."

"She saw me staring out the window."

I smiled. "So she knows you're here. Open the door."

Boyd opened it, and Carrie came in.

"Ivy was spying on you. I just glanced out," Boyd said.

Carrie laughed, sat on the couch, and smiled at me. "Thanks for making that happen."

"You aren't mad?"

"Not at all. José just asked me out."

Boyd bent down and picked up Creepers. "I should hope so."

"I've been hoping forever. I doubt he would have if you hadn't helped."

I smiled. "It's hard for me to mind my own business."

"It's a good thing," Boyd said. "Now Bill's behind bars."

I groaned. "Bill didn't kill Deputy Russell. It was Hanson."

"What? I would have sworn it was Bill."

"I thought so, but then I remembered something Hanson said that didn't fit with what he said later. It was him."

"Did he think it was Jett?"

"No. Russell just made him mad. He didn't mean to kill him. I still feel guilty it was at my booth and with my cake stand. If I had dealt with Hanson better, he might have gone home, and nothing would have happened."

"Don't blame yourself," Carrie said. "That's a dangerous thing. You didn't make his choices."

"I know."

"Did he give off signs when you dated him?" Boyd asked.

"We didn't date long, and part of it was because of his temper. He was never mean to me, but he would get so upset when things didn't go his way. He got lost once and punched the steering wheel so hard he broke his finger."

"Well, it's good it's taken care of."

Carrie grinned. "You put away a murder and got José to ask me out. So what's your next case?"

I clapped my hands together. "No case. I'm going to take some time to relax. I'll be back."

I hurried to my room and pulled the old letters from my dresser, then carried them back out. "I found these letters in Barbra's attic. I can't wait to read them."

Carrie bent over to see the pile. "They look old."

"I'm hoping they're love letters. I figure they are because why else keep them?"

"What's the name on them?" Boyd asked. "I might have known the people. I've been around since the dinosaurs."

"They don't have anything written on top." I sat down on the couch and untied the blue ribbon. The top letter had a fancy M that I hadn't seen because of the ribbon. "M. Did anyone live in Barbra's house that started with an M?"

Boyd sat next to me and scratched his head. "I'm not sure. The people who lived there before were the Mortensons. That starts with an M. I'm trying to think of their first names. It's been a while."

I opened the top letter. It wasn't sealed. I pulled out a yellowed paper and unfolded it. My eyes ran across the page, and I smiled. "It starts with dearest."

Carrie sat on the other side of me and looked over my shoulder.

I glanced down at the bottom. It was signed with an R. "Come on. No names."

"It's a forbidden love," Boyd said.

I giggled. "What makes you think that?"

He pointed at the paper. "It says, *You said your family wouldn't approve of you talking to an almost stranger.* It's a Romeo and Juliet thing."

"This is so exciting!" I said, trying to read the fancy cursive. "Do you think the writer is a man or a woman?"

"I can't tell," Carrie said. "Maybe once you start reading, you'll catch it by the context."

Someone pounded on the door, and we all looked up. "Come in!" I called.

José poked his head in. "One of the ovens went out."

I frowned. "Again?"

"We had another big group come in too. I'll call the repairman, but we might need to use your oven."

"I can help," Carrie said, jumping up. José smiled.

I couldn't even feel bummed about the oven when I saw the way they looked at each other. "Let me put these away, and I'll be down."

I tucked the letters safely away. I couldn't wait to figure out who M and R were, but it would have to be another time.

Chapter 20

The sun was setting, and I walked across town, holding Jett's hand. Jett held Conan's leash in his other hand, and the hyper little dog ran all over the sidewalk. We passed the big fenced-off area where they would build the new condos. A big billboard showed a picture of tan stucco condos with a couple smiling in the corner.

"The condos are going to change the town," Jett said. "I hope it's a good change. It might give us all a shock for a while as we adjust. It's going to strain our resources until we get it all figured out."

"Do you think the town will start growing?"

"Hopefully. The population's been going down for as long as I can remember. One hundred new living spaces should be huge around here."

"I'm ready for a quiet week," I said. "I don't think I'll ever go to the fair again."

"Do you have quiet weeks?" Jett teased.

"Not since I moved here. I have plans, though, and they don't involve snooping." I narrowed my eyes. "That's not exactly true. It depends on how you look at it."

Jett chuckled. "What does that mean?"

"I'm going to read the letters I found in Barbra's attic. It's some sort of forbidden love thing."

"Ah. Sounds like it's right up your alley. And the best part is, you can't get into trouble."

I bumped him playfully with my shoulder.

"Hanson confessed to everything," he said.

My smile slipped.

"I feel bad for him, to be honest. He shouldn't have done it, but he didn't mean for it to go the way it did. Still, he's not as sorry as he should be. He keeps bringing up the fact that Russell was a jerk."

"Did you ever find out who slashed your tire?"

"Brooke. She was doing everything she could to take the focus off Hanson. She did things when she knew he would have an alibi. She didn't think he was guilty, but she thought it looked like he was. Now that he's confessed, she doesn't want anything to do with him. Ledford took her to Wichita since we don't have enough cells, and I don't dare put Bill and Hanson together."

"I don't blame you."

"We also found Bill's hidden money. It's the money from Russell's house. He admitted to sneaking over and taking it. He said he figured it didn't matter since Russell was dead and some of the money was his."

Conan barked at a tree. He had more misguided energy than any dog I'd ever seen.

"Come on, boy," Jett said, gently pulling the leash. Conan barked happily and moved on.

We passed a campaign sign. It looked like Mayor Jepson was running again.

"Should you be putting up campaign signs?" I asked.

Jett shrugged. "I guess so. Leford decided not to run against me, so I'm not sure if there's a point. Not if there isn't another person running against me."

"It might be good to have your name out there for people. I can help."

"Thanks. I'll have to have some signs made. I can probably get away with two or three per town."

"You can put a huge one in the window at Sue's."

He grinned. "Because that won't scream, *My girlfriend owns this place!*"

"Does it matter? Everyone knows."

"No one's running against Mayor Jepson either."

"I still think Boyd should. I hate dealing with Mayor Jepson. Every time he reserves the party room, I die inside. He's reserved it for a day every week for the next month."

"He's probably trying to get votes by having parties."

"That's what it sounds like."

"I would encourage Boyd to run, but he's not what I would call qualified."

"He learns fast."

"True. Maybe I'll talk to him. If nothing else came of it, I could vote and not feel bad about myself after. Jepson doesn't have Muddy Creek's best interests on his agenda. He likes the popularity and the perks, but he doesn't do much."

"If he doesn't do much, what makes him qualified over Boyd? Boyd would try."

"True. Jepson wasn't qualified when he started, but no one around here is. Most people are farmers."

"Boyd would be perfect. He knows what life around here is like and could help the community because of it."

"He might not want to. He's retired after all."

"But he gets bored."

Jett smiled as we walked up to the diner. "If he became mayor, he might be too busy to get into trouble with you."

"Does being mayor give a person more resources? If so, he might be more helpful to me."

Jett groaned. "That might be worse."

I yawned as we walked around the diner. "How could it be worse?"

"You would probably make him help you illegally and get him thrown out of office."

"I don't think I would go that far. Hey, whatever happened with Fran? Did she go to jail?"

"No. I confiscated her plants. I won't be so easy on her if she does it again, and I'll keep a close eye on her. It turns out she got her seeds from Deputy Russell. I guess he was selling them to lots of people but then forcing them to pay him so he wouldn't tell."

"But he would get in more trouble than they would."

"Yeah, but people don't think clearly when they're being threatened."

Boyd's bike leaned against the stairs to my apartment.

Jett shook his head. "I'm surprised Boyd moved in with me and not you. He's here a lot."

"That's another reason he should run. He has a hard time filling his time, so he spends way more time with Creepers and Conan than he should. Creepers loves him, but sometimes he hides from him because he wants to chill and not be bothered."

We went into the apartment and found Boyd on the floor holding a cat toy. Creepers was nowhere in sight.

"It's about time you came," he said. "I can't get off the floor." I frowned and offered my hand. Maybe Boyd wasn't in good enough health to run for mayor. Jett and I pulled him up, and he stretched. "I could have gotten up if I had to, but I'm tired. I thought about falling asleep on the floor."

Jett nodded. "It's getting dark. I can go get my truck and take you home."

"I don't mind riding in the dark. It's peaceful." Conan ran around Boyd and pulled on his pant leg until Boyd bent down and patted his head. He walked over to the door and pulled it open. "Bye, Ivy. See you at home," he said, nodding at Jett.

"Let's see the letters," Jett said, sitting on the couch. Conan chased his tail and barked. Creepers came lazily out of my room and watched him.

I grabbed the letters and handed them to him. "They weren't mailed, so I don't know the date. They have to be at least thirty years old because that's how long Barbra's lived there."

"I'd guess they were older than that."

"I bet they are. I'm going to read them, then figure out who wrote them."

"You could look at county records to see who's lived here." Jett looked through all the envelopes. "This bottom one has an R instead of an M on it, and it's still sealed."

"Let me see." He handed me the bottom envelope, and I turned it. "So all of these were from R to M, but the last one must be from M to R. But it isn't opened, so R never saw it!"

He leaned forward. "Open it."

"No. I need to read them in order and save that one until last."

"You have more self-control than I do. I should probably go." He leaned over and kissed me, then stood. "I'll see you tomorrow."

I said goodbye and got ready for bed. The letters were calling out to me, but I was too tired to focus on the small cursive. I curled up in bed next to Creepers and smiled. The letters would be a fun puzzle and hopefully tell the story of two people's pasts.

Loaded Chicken and Potato Casserole

Ingredients:

- 1 lb chicken breast, cubed

- 6–8 medium red potatoes, cubed

- 1/3 cup olive oil

- 1 1/2 teaspoons salt

- 1 tablespoon paprika

- 2 tablespoons garlic powder

- 2 cups shredded fiesta blend cheese

- 1 cup cooked and crumbled bacon

Instructions:

1. Preheat oven to **400°F (200°C)**.

2. Spray a **9x13-inch** baking dish with nonstick cooking spray.

3. In a large bowl, whisk together the olive oil, salt, paprika, and garlic powder.

4. Add the cubed potatoes and chicken to the bowl

and toss until well coated.

5. Pour the mixture into the prepared baking dish.

6. Bake for **60 minutes**, stirring every **20 minutes** to ensure even cooking.

7. While the casserole bakes, cook the bacon until crispy. Crumble or chop into pieces.

8. Once the chicken and potatoes are fully cooked and golden, remove the dish from the oven.

9. Sprinkle the shredded cheese evenly over the top, followed by the crumbled bacon.

10. Return the dish to the oven and bake for an additional **5 minutes**, or until the cheese is melted and bubbly.

11. Let cool slightly before serving.

Also By Kristy Dixon

<u>Cozy Mystery</u>
Murder With a Side of Bacon
Murder With a Hint of Cinnamon
Murder With a Fudge Brownie to Go
Murder With a Splash of Vanilla
Murder With a Drizzle of Syrup

<u>Young Adult</u>
The Silver Eclipse (3 books)
The Amethyst Crown
More Than Once Upon a Time

Trapped In Once Upon a Time
The Beginning of Once Upon a Time
Riviand Lost (4 books)

<u>Coming Soon!</u>
Murder With a Bite of Biscotti
Forgotten in Once Upon a Time
Rise of the Serpent (Riviand Lost Book 5)

About the Author

Kristy Dixon started writing stories when she was seven and never stopped. She enjoys writing cozy mysteries and YA. At home, she spends her time playing board games with her husband and kids and writing. Occasionally she takes part in a Super Mario marathon. She has six chickens and a cat that help keep life amusing. If she isn't playing with her kids or writing, she is usually eating cookies, or wishing she was eating cookies.